HAI … VINNER OF
THE … THE MOST
PRE … WORLD OF
SCII …

'Harlan Ellison is a man on the move, and he is moving fast . . . colourful, intrusive, abrasive, irritating, hilarious, illogical, inconsistent, unpredictable, and one hell of a writer. Watch him.' *Theodore Sturgeon*

'Harlan Ellison is a true virtuoso.' *Publishers' Weekly*

'Harlan Ellison is a phenomenon, *sui generis* . . . and I recommend the experience heartily to anyone with a strong stomach for emotions and a mind open to some fabulous fantasy tripping.' *Los Angeles Times*

Harlan Ellison

All the Sounds of Fear

Panther

Granada Publishing Limited
First published in 1973 by Panther Books Ltd
Park Street, St Albans, Herts

Made and printed in Great Britain by
Richard Clay (The Chaucer Press) Ltd,
Bungay, Suffolk
Set in Linotype Times
Australia—recommended price only
Acknowledgments
'I Have No Mouth, and I Must Scream' appeared in *If: Worlds of Science Fiction* for March, 1967. Copyright 1967 by Galaxy Publishing Corporation: all rights returned to author, 1968.
'The Discarded' (under the title 'The Abnormals') appeared in *Fantastic* for April 1959. Copyright 1959 by Ziff-Davis Publishing Company.
'Deeper Than the Darkness' appeared in *Infinity Science Fiction* for April 1957. Copyright 1957 by Royal Publications, Inc.
'Blind Lightning' appeared in *Fantastic Universe Science Fiction* for June 1956. Copyright 1956 by King-Size Publications, Inc.
'All the Sounds of Fear' appeared in *The Saint Detective Magazine* (French and British editions). Copyright 1962 by Fiction Publishing Company. Copyright 1962 by Harlan Ellison in the United States: reprinted from *Ellison Wonderland* by permission of the author, his agent, and Paperback Library, Inc.
'The Silver Corridor' appeared in *Infinity Science Fiction* for October, 1956. Copyright 1956 by Royal Publications, Inc.
'"Repent, Harlequin!" Said the Ticktockman' appeared in *Galaxy* for December 1965. Copyright, New York, 1965 by Galaxy Publishing Corporation.
'Bright Eyes' appeared in *Fantastic* for April 1965. Copyright 1965 by Ziff-Davis Publishing Company.

This book is dedicated to the memory of
EVELYN DEL REY,
a dear friend, for laughter and for caring . . .

And to the memories of:
ALLISON KRAUSE
JEFFREY GLEN MILLER
WILLIAM K. SCHROEDER
SANDRA LEE SHEUER

four Kent State University students senselessly murdered in their society's final act of alienation.
The list is incomplete. There are many others. There will be more.

Contents

Introduction: The Song of the Soul

Carl Jung once said, 'The only thing we have to fear on this planet is man.' He could not have been more correct. We have only to look around us, at the fissures in the rock-wall of our times, to know that we have created for ourselves a madhouse of irrationality and despair. The lunacies of our world erupt daily like boils on the diseased body of civilization. Is it, hopefully, the re-awakening of conscience, or, more likely the refracted pain of denying our souls?

Alienation.

The keyword so easily bandied by sociologists and inept novelists alike. The explanation for racial strife, random violence, mass madness, the rape of our planet. Man feels cut off. He feels denied. He feels alone. He is alienated.

If one more quotation might be permitted, the words of Oscar Wilde—himself a classic study of alienation—serve to describe alienation: 'To reject one's own experiences is to arrest one's own development. To deny one's own experience is to put a lie into the lips of one's own life. It is no less than a denial of the Soul.'

Alone against his world, the man of today finds his gods have deserted him, his brother has grown fangs, the machine clatters ever nearer on his heels, fear is the only lover demanding his clasp, and without answers he turns and turns, and finds only darkness.

The creative intellect struggles against this sorry reality. Pressing with unflagging intensity against the shuddering membrane of alienation, against the interface between himself and freedom of the soul, the artist tries to gain an exit with the magics of words and movements and colors. Yet all around him the inexorable inertia of the alienated society finds the strength to keep rolling, grinding, crushing. It would seem only the mind of the madman is free.

And even so, the artist persists. He speaks of man, alone in the night, alone against the stars, alone against tomorrow—more starless and darker than even today. He speaks of worlds beyond our world, days beyond our days, places crosswhen and never-will-be, in hopes that cautions may be flung on the wind and somehow still be heard.

These are stories I have written over the past ten years and more. Stories in which the theme of alienation dominates. They are by no means stories of hopelessness; for in examples of the damned and lost, we find hope within ourselves. Alienated, perhaps; yet never alone.

HARLAN ELLISON
Los Angeles, January, 1970

I Have No Mouth, and I Must Scream

Limp, the body of Gorrister hung from the pink palette; unsupported—hanging high above us in the computer chamber; and it did not shiver in the chill, oily breeze that blew eternally through the main cavern. The body hung head down, attached to the underside of the palette by the sole of its right foot. It had been drained of blood through a precise incision made from ear to ear under the lantern jaw. There was no blood on the reflective surface of the metal floor.

When Gorrister joined our group and looked up at himself, it was already too late for us to realize that once again AM had duped us, had had his fun; it had been a diversion on the part of the machine. Three of us had vomited, turning away from one another in a reflex as ancient as the nausea that had produced it.

Gorrister went white. It was almost as though he had seen a voodoo fetish, and was afraid for the future. 'Oh God,' he mumbled, and walked away. The three of us followed him after a time, and found him sitting with his back to one of the smaller chittering banks, his head in his hands. Ellen knelt down beside him and stroked his hair. He didn't move, but his voice came out of his covered face quite clearly. 'Why doesn't it just do-us-in and get it over with? Christ, I don't know how much longer I can go on like this.'

It was our one hundred and ninth year in the computer.

He was speaking for all of us.

Nimdok (which was the name the machine had forced him to use, because it liked to amuse itself with strange sounds) hallucinated that there were canned goods in the ice caverns. Gorrister and I were very dubious. 'It's another shuck,' I told them. 'Like the goddam frozen elephant it sold us. Benny almost went out of his mind over *that* one. We'll hike all that way and it'll be putrified or some damn thing. I say forget it. Stay here; it'll have to come up with something pretty soon or we'll die.'

Benny shrugged. Three days it had been since we'd last eaten. Worms. Thick, ropey.

Nimdok was no more certain. He knew there was the chance, but he was getting thin. It couldn't be any worse there, than here. Colder, but that didn't matter much. Hot, cold, raining, lava, boils or locust—it never mattered: the machine masturbated and we had to take it or die.

Ellen decided us. 'I've got to have something, Ted. Maybe there'll be some Bartlett pears or peaches. Please, Ted, let's try it.'

I gave in easily. What the hell. Mattered not at all. Ellen was grateful, though. She took me twice out of turn. Even that had ceased to matter. The machine giggled every time we did it. Loud, up there, back there, all around us. And she never climaxed, so why bother.

We left on a Thursday. The machine always kept us up-to-date on the date. The passage of time was important; not to us sure as hell, but to it. Thursday. Thanks.

Nimdok and Gorrister carried Ellen for a while, their hands locked to their own and each other's wrists, a seat. Benny and I walked before and after, just to make sure that if anything happened, it would catch one of us and at least Ellen would be safe. Fat chance, safe. Didn't matter.

It was only a hundred miles or so to the ice caverns, and on the second day, when we were lying out under the blistering sun-thing it had materialized, it sent down some manna. Tasted like boiled boar urine. We ate it.

On the third day we passed through a valley of obsolescence, filled with rusting carcasses of ancient computer banks. AM had been as ruthless with his own life as with ours. It was a mark of his personality: he strove for perfection. Whether it was a matter of killing off unproductive elements in his own world-filling bulk, or perfecting methods for torturing us, AM was as thorough as those who had invented him—now long-since gone to dust—could ever have hoped.

There was light filtering down from above, and we realized we must be very near the surface. But we didn't try to crawl up to see. There was virtually nothing out there; had been nothing that could be considered anything for over a hundred years. Only the blasted skin of what had once been the home of billions. Now there were only the five of us, down here inside, alone with AM.

I heard Ellen saying, frantically, 'No, Benny! Don't, come on, Benny, don't please!'

And then I realized I had been hearing Benny murmuring, under his breath, for several minutes. He was saying, 'I'm gonna get out, I'm gonna get out . . .' over and over. His monkeylike face was crumbled up in an expression of beatific delight and sadness, all at the same time. The radiation scars AM had given him during the 'festival' were drawn down into a mass of pink-white puckerings, and his features seemed to work independently of one another. Perhaps Benny was the luckiest of the five of us: he had gone stark, staring mad many years before.

But even though we could call AM any damned thing we liked, could think the foulest thoughts of fused memory banks and corroded base plates, of burnt out circuits and shattered control bubbles, the machine would not tolerate our trying to escape. Benny leaped away from me as I made a grab for him. He scrambled up the face of a smaller memory cube, tilted on its side and filled with rotted components. He squatted there for a moment, looking like the chimpanzee AM had intended him to resemble.

Then he leaped high, caught a trailing beam of pitted and corroded metal, and went up it, hand over hand like an animal, till he was on a girdered ledge, twenty feet above us.

'Oh, Ted, Nimdok, please, help him, get him down before——' She cut off. Tears began to stand in her eyes. She moved her hands aimlessly.

It was too late. None of us wanted to be near him, when whatever was going to happen, happened. And besides, we all saw through her concern. When AM had altered Benny, during his mad period, it was not merely his face he had made like a giant ape. He was big in the privates, she loved that! She serviced us, as a matter of course, but she loved it from him. Oh Ellen, pedestal Ellen, pristine pure Ellen, oh Ellen the clean! Scum filth.

Gorrister slapped her. She slumped down, staring up at poor loonie Benny, and she cried. It was her big defense, crying. We had gotten used to it seventy-five years ago. Gorrister kicked her in the side.

Then the sound began. It was light, that sound. Half sound and half light, something that began to glow from Benny's eyes, and pulse with growing loudness, dim sonorities that grew more gigantic and brighter as the light/sound increased in tempo. It must have been painful, and the pain must have been increasing with the boldness of the light, the rising volume of the sound, for Benny began to mewl like a wounded animal. At first softly, when the light was dim and the sound was muted, then louder as his shoulders hunched together, his back humped, as though he were trying to get away from it. His hands folded across his chest like a chipmunk's. His head tilted to the side. The sad little monkey-face pinched in anguish. Then he began to howl, as the sound coming from his eyes grew louder. Louder and louder. I slapped the sides of my head with my hands, but I couldn't shut it out, it cut through easily. The pain shivered through my flesh like tinfoil on a tooth.

And Benny was suddenly pulled erect. On the girder he stood up, jerked to his feet like a puppet. The light was now pulsing out of his eyes in two great round beams. The sound crawled up and up some incomprehensible scale, and then he fell forward, straight down, and hit the plate steel floor with a crash. He lay there jerking spastically as the light flowed around and around him and the sound spiraled up out of normal range.

Then the light beat its way back inside his head, the sound spiraled down, and he was left lying there, crying piteously.

His eyes were two soft, moist pools of pus-like jelly. AM had blinded him. Gorrister and Nimdok and myself . . . we turned away. But not before we caught the look of relief on Ellen's warm, concerned face.

Sea-green light suffused the cavern where we made camp. AM provided punk and we burned it, sitting huddled around the wan and pathetic fire, telling stories to keep Benny from crying in his permanent night.

'What does AM mean?'

Gorrister answered him. We had done this sequence a thousand times before, and it was familiar to Benny. 'At first it meant Allied Mastercomputer, and then it meant Adaptive Manipulator, and later on it developed sentience and linked itself up and they called it an Aggressive Menace; but by then it was too late; and finally it called *itself* AM, emerging intelligence, and what it meant was I am ... *cogito ergo sum* ... I think, therefore I am.'

Benny drooled a little, and snickered.

'There was the Chinese AM and the Russian AM and the Yankee AM and——' He stopped. Benny was beating on the floorplates with a large, hard fist. He was not happy. Gorrister had not started at the beginning.

Gorrister began again. 'The Cold War started and became World War Three and just kept going. It became a big war, a very complex war, so they needed the computers to handle it. They sank the first shafts and began building AM. There was the Chinese AM and the Russian AM and the Yankee AM and everything was fine until they had honeycombed the entire planet, adding on this element and that element. But one day AM woke up and knew who he was, and he linked himself, and he began feeding all the killing data, until everyone was dead, except for the five of us, and AM brought us down here.'

Benny was smiling sadly. He was also drooling again. Ellen wiped the spittle from the corner of his mouth with the hem of her skirt. Gorrister always tried to tell it a little more succinctly each time, but beyond the bare facts there was nothing to say. None of us knew why AM had saved five people, or why our specific five, or why he spent all his time tormenting us, nor even why he had made us virtually immortal...

In the darkness, one of the computer banks began humming. The tone was picked up half a mile away down the cavern by another bank. Then one by one, each of the elements began to tune itself, and there was a faint chittering as thought raced through the machine.

The sound grew, and the lights ran across the faces of the consoles like heat lightning. The sound spiraled up till it sounded like a million metallic insects, angry, menacing.

'What is it?' Ellen cried. There was terror in her voice. She hadn't become accustomed to it, even now.

'It's going to be bad this time,' Nimdok said.

'He's going to speak,' Gorrister ventured.

'Let's get the hell out of here!' I said suddenly, getting to my feet.

'No, Ted, sit down ... what if he's got pits out there, or something else, we can't see, it's too dark.' Gorrister said it with resignation.

Then we heard ... I don't know...

Something moving toward us in the darkness. Huge, shambling, hairy, moist, it came toward us. We couldn't even see it, but there was the ponderous impression of *bulk*, heaving itself toward us. Great weight was coming at us, out of the darkness, and it was more a sense of *pressure*, of air forcing itself into a limited space, expanding the invisible walls of a sphere. Benny began to whimper. Nimdok's lower lip trembled and he bit it hard, trying to stop it. Ellen slid across the metal floor to Gorrister and huddled into him. There was the smell of matted, wet fur in the cavern. There was the smell of charred wood. There was the smell of dusty velvet. There was the smell of rotting orchids. There was the smell of sour milk. There was the smell of sulphur, of rancid butter, of oil slick, of grease, of chalk dust, of human scalps.

AM was keying us. He was tickling us. There was the smell of——

I heard myself shriek, and the hinges of my jaw ached. I scuttled across the floor, across the cold metal with its endless lines of rivets, on my hands and knees, the smell gagging me, filling my head with a thunderous pain that sent me away in horror. I fled like a cockroach, across the floor and out into the darkness, that *something* moving inexorably after me. The others were still back there, gathered around the firelight, laughing ... their hysterical choir of insane giggles rising up into the darkness like thick, many-colored wood smoke. I went away, quickly, and hid.

How many hours it may have been, how many days or even years, they never told me. Ellen chided me for 'sulking' and Nimdok tried to persuade me it had only been a nervous reflex on their part—the laughing.

But I knew it wasn't the relief a soldier feels when the bullet hits the man next to him. I knew it wasn't a reflex. They hated me. They were surely against me, and AM could even sense this hatred, and made it worse for me *because of* the depth of their hatred. We had been kept alive, rejuvenated, made to remain constantly at the age we had been when AM had brought us below, and they hated me because I was the youngest, and the one AM had affected least of all.

I knew. God, how I knew. The bastards, and that dirty bitch Ellen. Benny had been a brilliant theorist, a college professor; now he was little more than a semi-human, semi-simian. He had been handsome, the machine had ruined that. He had been lucid, the machine had driven him mad. He had been gay, and the machine had given him an organ fit for a horse. AM had done a job on Benny. Gorrister had been a worrier. He was a connie, a conscientious objector; he was a peace marcher; he was a planner, a doer, a looker-ahead. AM had turned him into a shoulder-shrugger, had made him a little dead in his concern. AM had robbed him. Nimdok went off in the darkness by himself for long times. I don't know what it was he did out there, AM never let us know. But whatever it was, Nimdok always came back white, drained of blood, shaken, shaking. AM had hit him hard in a special way, even if we didn't know quite how. And Ellen. That douche bag! AM had left her alone; had made her more of a slut than she had ever been. All her talk of sweetness and light, all her memories of true love, all the lies she wanted us to believe that she had been a virgin only twice removed before AM grabbed her and brought her down here with us. It was all filth, that lady my lady Ellen. She loved it, five men all to herself. No, AM had given her pleasure, even if she said it wasn't nice to do.

I was the only one still sane and whole.

AM had not tampered with *my* mind.

I only had to suffer what he visited down on us. All the delusions, all the nightmares, the torments. But those scum, all four of them, they were lined and arrayed against me. If I hadn't had to stand them off all the time, be on my guard against them all the time, I might have found it easier to combat AM.

At which point it passed, and I began crying.

Oh, Jesus sweet Jesus, if there ever was a Jesus and if there is a God, please please please let us out of here, or kill us. Because at that moment I think I realized completely, so that I was able to verbalize it: AM was intent on keeping us in his belly forever, twisting and torturing us forever. The machine hated us as no sentient creature had ever hated before. And we were helpless. It also became hideously clear:

If there was a sweet Jesus and if there was a God, the God was AM.

The hurricane hit us with the force of a glacier thundering into the sea. It was a palpable presence. Winds that tore at us, flinging us back the way we had come, down the twisting, computer-lined corridors of the darkway. Ellen screamed as she was lifted and hurled face-forward into a screaming shoal of machines, their individual voices strident as bats in flight. She could not even fall. The howling wind kept her aloft, buffetted her, bounced her, tossed her back and back and down away from us, out of sight suddenly as she was swirled around a bend in the darkway. Her face had been bloody, her eyes closed.

None of us could get to her. We clung tenaciously to whatever outcropping we had reached: Benny wedged in between two great crackle-finish cabinets, Nimdok with fingers claw-formed over a railing circling a catwalk forty feet above us, Gorrister plastered upside-down against a wall niche formed by two great machines with glass-faced dials that swung back and forth between red and yellow lines whose meanings we could not even fathom.

Sliding across the deckplates, the tips of my fingers had been ripped away. I was trembling, shuddering, rocking as the wind beat at me, whipped at me, screamed down out of nowhere at me and pulled me free from one sliver-thin opening in the plates to the next. My mind was a roiling tinkling sucksounding softness of brain parts that expanded and contracted in quivering frenzy.

The wind was the scream of a great mad bird, as it

flapped its immense wings.

And then we were all lifted and hurled away from there, down back the way we had come, around a bend, into a darkway we had never explored, over terrain that was ruined and filled with broken glass and rotting cables and rusted metal and far away farther than any of us had ever been . . .

Trailing along miles behind Ellen, I could see her every now and then, crashing into metal walls and surging on, with all of us screaming in the freezing, thunderous hurricane wind that would never end and then suddenly it stopped and we fell. We had been in flight for an endless time. I thought it might have been weeks. We fell, and hit, and I went through red and gray and black and heard myself moaning. Not dead.

AM went into my mind. He walked smoothly here and there, and looked with interest at all the pock marks he had created in one hundred and nine years. He looked at the cross-routed and reconnected synapses and all the tissue damage his gift of immortality had included. He smiled softly at the pit that dropped into the center of my brain and the faint, moth-soft murmurings of the things far down there gibbered without meaning, without pause. AM said, very politely, in a pillar of stainless steel and neon letters:

HATE. LET ME TELL
YOU HOW MUCH I'VE
COME TO HATE YOU
SINCE I BEGAN TO
LIVE. THERE ARE
387.44 MILLION
MILES OF PRINTED

CIRCUITS IN WAFER
THIN LAYERS THAT
FILL MY COMPLEX.
IF THE WORD HATE
WAS ENGRAVED ON
EACH NANOANGSTROM
OF THOSE HUNDREDS
OF MILLION MILES
IT WOULD NOT EQUAL
ONE ONE-BILLIONTH
OF THE HATE I FEEL
FOR HUMANS AT THIS
MICRO-INSTANT FOR
YOU. HATE. HATE.

AM said it with the sliding cold horror of a razor blade slicing my eyeball. AM said it with the bubbling thickness of my lungs filling with phlegm, drowning me from within. AM said it with the shriek of babies being ground beneath blue-hot rollers. AM said it with the taste of maggoty pork. AM touched me in every way I had ever been touched, and devised new ways, at his leisure, there inside my mind.

All to bring me to full realization of why he had done this to the five of us; why he had saved us for himself.

We had given him sentience. Inadvertently, of course, but sentience nonetheless. But he had been trapped. He was a machine. We had allowed him to think, but to do nothing with it. In rage, in frenzy, he had killed us, almost all of us, and still he was trapped. He could not wander, he could not wonder, he could not belong. He could merely be. And so, with the innate loathing that all machines had always held for the weak, soft creatures who had built them, he had sought revenge. And in his paranoia, he had decided to reprieve five of us, for a personal, everlasting punishment that would never serve to diminish his hatred ... that would merely keep him reminded, amused, proficient at hating man. Immortal, trapped, subject to any torment he could devise for us from the limitless miracles at his command.

He would never let us go. We were his belly slaves. We were all he had to do with his forever time. We would be forever with him, with the cavern-filling bulk of him, with the all-mind soulless world he had become. He was Earth and we were the fruit of that Earth and though he had eaten us, he would never digest us. We could not die. We had tried it. We had attempted suicide, oh one or two of us had. But AM had stopped us. I suppose we had wanted to be stopped.

Don't ask why. I never did. More than a million times a day. Perhaps once we might be able to sneak a death past him. Immortal, yes, but not indestructible. I saw that when AM withdrew from my mind, and allowed me the exquisite ugliness of returning to consciousness with the feeling of that burning neon pillar still rammed deep into the soft gray brain matter.

He withdrew murmuring *to hell with you.*

And added, brightly, *but then you're there, aren't you.*

The huricane had, indeed, precisely, been caused by a great mad bird, as it flapped its immense wings.

We had been traveling for close to a month, and AM had allowed passages to open to us only sufficient to lead us up there, directly under the North Pole, where he had nightmared the creature for our torment. What whole cloth had he employed to create such a beast? Where had he gotten the concept? From our minds? From his knowledge of everything that had ever been on this planet he now infested and ruled? From Norse mythology it had sprung, this eagle, this carrion bird, this roc, this Huergelmir. The wind creature. Hurakan incarnate.

Gigantic. The words immense, monstrous, grotesque, massive, swollen, overpowering, beyond description. There on a mound rising above us, the bird of winds heaved with its own irregular breathing, its snake neck arching up into the gloom beneath the North Pole, supporting a head as large as a Tudor mansion; a beak that opened slowly as the jaws of the most monstrous crocodile ever conceived, sensuously; ridges of tufted flesh puckered about two evil eyes, as cold as the view down into a glacial crevasse, ice blue and somehow moving liquidly; it heaved once more, and lifted its great sweat-colored wings in a movement that was certainly a shrug. Then it settled and slept. Talons. Fangs. Nails. Blades. It slept.

AM appeared to us as a burning bush and said we could kill the hurricane bird if we wanted to eat. We had not eaten in a very long time, but even so, Gorrister merely shrugged. Benny began to shiver and he drooled. Ellen held him. 'Ted, I'm hungry,' she said. I smiled at her; I was trying to be reassuring. But it was as phony as Nimdok's bravado: 'Give us weapons!' he demanded.

The burning bush vanished and there were two crude sets of bow and arrows, and a water pistol, lying on the cold deckplates. I picked up a set. Useless.

Nimdok swallowed heavily. We turned and started the long way back. The hurricane bird had blown us about for a length of time we could not conceive. Most of that time we had been unconscious. But we had not eaten. A month on the march to the bird itself. Without food. Now how much longer to find our way to the ice caverns, and the promised canned goods?

None of us cared to think about it. We would not die. We would be given filths and scums to eat, of one kind or another. Or nothing at all. AM would keep our bodies alive somehow, in pain, in agony.

The bird slept back there, for how long it didn't matter; when AM was tired of its being there, it would vanish. But all that meat. All that tender meat.

As we walked, the lunatic laugh of a fat woman rang high and around us in the computer chambers that led endlessly nowhere.

It was not Ellen's laugh. She was not fat, and I had not heard her laugh for one hundred and nine years. In fact, I had not heard . . . we walked . . . I was hungry . . .

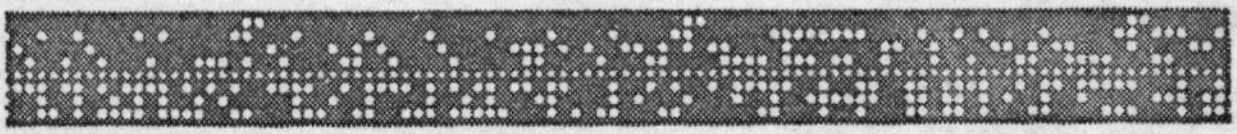

We moved slowly. There was often fainting, and we would have to wait. One day he decided to cause an earthquake, at the same time rooting us to the spot with nails through the soft pads of our feet. Ellen and Nimdok were both caught when a fissure shot its lightning-bolt opening across the floorplates. They disappeared and were gone. When the earthquake was over we continued on our way, Benny, Gorrister, and myself. Ellen and Nimdok were returned to us later that night which became a day abruptly as the heavenly legion bore them to us with a celestial chorus singing, 'Go Down Moses.' The archangels circled several times and then dropped the hideously mangled bodies. We kept walking, and a while later Ellen and Nimdok fell in behind us. They were no worse for wear.

But now Ellen walked with a limp. AM had left her that.

It was a long trip to the ice caverns, to find the canned food. Ellen kept talking about Bing cherries and Hawaiian fruit cocktail. I tried not to think about it. The hunger was something that had come to life, even as AM had come to life. It was alive in my belly, even as we were alive in the belly of AM, and AM was alive in the belly of the Earth, and AM wanted the similarity known to us. So he heightened the hunger. There was no way to describe the pains that not having eaten for months brought us. And yet we were kept alive. Stomachs that were merely cauldrons of acid, bubbling, foaming, always shooting spears of sliver-thin pain into our chests. It was the pain of the terminal ulcer, terminal cancer, terminal paresis. It was unending pain . . .

And we passed through the cavern of rats.

And we passed through the path of boiling steam.

And we passed through the country of the blind.

And we passed through the slough of despond.

And we passed through the vale of tears.

And we came, finally, to the ice caverns. Horizonless thousands of miles in which the ice had formed in blue and silver flashes, where novas lived in the glass. The chill downdropping stalactites as thick and glorious as diamonds that had been made to run like jelly and then solidified in graceful eternities of smooth, sharp perfection.

We saw the stack of canned goods, and we tried to run to them. We fell in the snow, and we got up and went on, and Benny shoved us away and went at them, and pawed them and gummed them and gnawed at them and he could not open them. AM had not given us a tool to open the cans.

Benny grabbed a three-quart can of guava shells, and began to batter it against the ice bank. The ice flew and shattered, but the can was merely dented while we heard the laughter of a fat lady, high overhead and echoing down and down and down the tundra. Benny went completely mad with rage. He began throwing cans, as we all scrabbled about in the snow and ice trying to find a way to end the helpless agony of frustration. There was no way.

Then Benny's mouth began to drool, and he flung himself on Gorrister . . .

In that instant, I went terribly calm.

Surrounded by madness, surrounded by hunger, surrounded by everything but death, I knew death was our only way out. AM had kept us alive, but there was a way to defeat him. Not total defeat, but at least peace. I would settle for that.

I had to do it quickly.

Benny was eating Gorrister's face. Gorrister on his side, thrashing snow, Benny wrapped around him with powerful monkey legs crushing Gorrister's waist, his hands locked around Gorrister's head like a nutcracker, and his mouth ripping at the tender skin of Gorrister's cheek. Gorrister screamed with such jagged-edged violence that stalactites fell; they plunged down softly, erect in the receiving snowdrifts. Spears, hundreds of them, everywhere, protruding from the snow. Benny's head pulled back sharply, as something gave all at once, and a bleeding raw-white dripping of flesh hung from his teeth.

Ellen's face, black against the white snow, dominos in chalk-dust. Nimdok with no expression but eyes, all eyes. Gorrister half-conscious. Benny now an animal. I knew AM would let him play. Gorrister would not die, but Benny would fill his stomach. I turned half to my right and drew a huge ice-spear from the snow.

All in an instant:

I drove the great ice-point ahead of me like a battering ram, braced against my right thigh. It struck Benny on the right side, just under the rib cage, and drove upward through his stomach and broke inside him. He pitched forward and lay still. Gorrister lay on his back, I pulled another spear free and straddled him, still moving, driving the spear straight down through his throat. His eyes closed as the cold penetrated. Ellen must have realized what I had decided, even as the fear gripped her. She ran at Nimdok with a short icicle, as he screamed, and into his mouth, and the force of her rush did the job. His head jerked sharply as if it had been nailed to the snow crust behind him.

All in an instant.

There was an eternity beat of soundless anticipation. I could hear AM draw in his breath. His toys had been taken from him. Three of them were dead, could not be revived. He could keep us alive, by his strength and his talent, but he was *not* God. He could not bring them back.

Ellen looked at me, her ebony features stark against the snow that surrounded us. There was fear and pleading in her manner, the way she held herself ready. I knew we had only a heartbeat before AM would stop us.

It struck her and she folded toward me, bleeding from the mouth. I could not read meaning into her expression, the pain had been too great, had contorted her face; but it *might* have been thank you. It's possible. Please.

Some hundreds of years may have passed. I don't know. AM has been having fun for some time, accelerating and retarding my time sense. I will say the word 'now'. *Now*. It took me ten months to say 'now.' I don't know. I *think* it has been some hundreds of years.

He was furious. He wouldn't let me bury them. It didn't matter. There was no way to dig in the deckplates. He dried up the snow. He brought the night. He roared and sent locusts. It didn't do a thing; they stayed dead. I'd had him. He was furious. I had thought AM hated me before. I was wrong. It is not even a shadow of the hate he now slavers from every printed circuit. He made certain I would suffer eternally and could not do myself in.

He left my mind intact. I can dream, I can wonder, I can lament. I remember all four of them. I wish——

Well, it doesn't make any sense. I know I saved them, I know I saved them from what has happened to me, but still, I cannot forget killing them. Ellen's face. It isn't easy. Sometimes I want to, it doesn't matter.

AM has altered me for his own peace of mind, I suppose. He doesn't want me to run at full speed into a computer bank and smash my skull. Or hold my breath till I faint. Or cut my throat on a rusted sheet of metal. There are reflective surfaces down here. I will describe myself as I see myself:

I am a great soft jelly thing. Smoothly rounded, with no mouth, with pulsing white holes filled by fog where my eyes used to be. Rubbery appendages that were once my arms; bulks rounding down into legless humps of soft slippery matter. I leave a moist trail when I move. Blotches of diseased, evil gray come and go on my surface, as though light is being beamed from within.

Outwardly: dumbly, I shamble about, a thing that could never have been known as human, a thing whose shape is so alien a travesty, that humanity becomes more obscene for the vague resemblance.

Inwardly: alone. Here. Living under the land, under the sea, in the belly of AM, whom we created because our time was badly spent and we must have known unconsciously that he could do it better. At least the four of them are safe at last.

AM will be all the madder for that. It makes me a little happier. And yet ... AM has won, simply ... he has taken his revenge ...

I have no mouth. And I must scream.

The Discarded

Bedzyk saw Riila go mad, and watched her throw herself against the lucite port, till her pinhead was a red blotch of pulped flesh and blood. He sighed, and sucked deeply from his massive bellows chest, and wondered how *he*, of all the Discards, had been silently nominated the leader. The ship hung in space, between the Moon and Earth, unwanted, unnoticed, a raft adrift in the sea of night.

Around him in the ship's saloon, the others watched Riila killing herself, and when her body fell to the rug, they turned away, allowing Bedzyk his choice of who was to dispose of her. He chose John Smith—the one with feathers where hair should have been—and the nameless one who clanged instead of talking.

The two of them lifted her heavy body, with its tiny pea of head, and carried it to the garbage port. They emptied it, opened it, tossed her inside, redogged and blew her out. She floated past the saloon window on her way sunward. In a moment she was lost.

Bedzyk sat down in a deep chair and drew breath whistlingly into his mighty chest. It was a chore, being leader of these people.

People? No, that was certainly not the word. These Discards. That was a fine willowy word to use. They were scrap, refuse, waste, garbage themselves. How fitting for Riila to have gone that way, out the garbage port. They would *all* bid goodbye that way some day. He noted there was no 'day' on the ship. But some good *something*—maybe day, maybe night—each of them would go sucking out that port like the garbage.

It had to be that way. They were Discards.

But people? No, they were not people. People did not have hooks where hands should have been, nor one eye, nor carapaces, nor humps on chests and backs, nor fins, nor any of the other mutations these residents of the ship sported. People were normal. Evenly matched sets of arms and legs and eyes. Evenly matched husbands, wives. Evenly distributed throughout the Solar System, and evenly dividing the goods of the System between themselves and the frontier worlds at the Edge. And all happily disposed to let the obscene Discards die in their prison ship.

'She's gone.'

He had pursed his lips, had sunk his perfectly normal head onto his gigantic chest, and had been thinking. Now he looked up at the speaker. It was John Smith, with feathers where hair should have been.

'I said: she's gone.'

Bedzyk nodded without replying. Riila had been just one more in the tradition. They had already lost over two hundred Discards from the ship. There would be more.

Strange how these—he hesitated again to use the word *people*, finally settled on the word they used among themselves: creatures—these *creatures* had steeled themselves to the death of one of their kind. Or perhaps they did not consider the rest as malformed as themselves. Each person on the ship was different. No two had been affected by Sickness in the same way. The very fibers of the muscles had altered with some of these creatures, making their limbs useless; on others the pores had clogged on their skin surfaces, eliminating all hair. On still others strange juices had been secreted in the blood stream, causing weird growths to erupt where smoothness had been. But perhaps each one thought he was less hideous than the others. It was conceivable. Bedzyk knew his great chest was not nearly as unpleasant to look upon as, say, Samswope's spiny crest and twin heads. *In fact,* Bedzyk mused wryly, *many people might think it was becoming, this great wedge of a chest, all matted with dark hair and heroic-seeming. Uh-huh, the others are pretty miserable to look at, but not me, especially.* Yes, it was conceivable.

In any case, they paid no attention now, if one of their group killed himself. They turned away; most of them were better off dead, anyhow.

Then he caught himself.

He was starting to get like the rest of them! He had to stop thinking like that. It wasn't right. No one should be allowed to take death like that. He resolved, the next one would be stopped, and he would deliver them a stern warning, and tell the Discards that they would find landfall soon, and to buck up.

But he knew he would sit and watch the next time, as he had this time. For he had made the same resolve before Riila had gone.

Samswope came into the saloon—he had been on KP all 'day' and both his heads were dripping with sweat—and picked his way among the conversing groups of Discards to the seat beside Bedzyk.

'Mmm.' It was a greeting; he was identifying his arrival.

'Hi, Sam. How was it?'

'Metsoo-metz,' he gibed, imitating Scalomina (the one-eyed ex-plumber, of Sicilian descent), tipping his hand in an obvious Scalominian gesture. 'I'll live. Unfortunately.' He added the last word with only a little drop of humor.

'Did I ever tell you the one about the Candy-Ass

Canadian Boil-Sucker?' He didn't even smile as he said it; with either head. Bedzyk nodded wearily: he didn't want to play that game. 'Yeah, well,' Samswope said wearily. He sat silently for several long moments, then added, with irony, 'But did I tell you I was married to her?' His wife had turned him in.

Morbidity ran knee-deep on the ship.

'Riila killed herself a little bit ago,' Bedzyk said carelessly. There was no other way to say it.

'I figured as much,' Samswope explained. 'I saw them carrying her past the galley to the garbage lock. That's number six this week alone. You going to do anything, Bedzyk?'

Bedzyk twisted abruptly in his chair. He leveled a gaze at a spot directly between Samswope's two heads. His words were bitter with helplessness and anger that the burden should be placed upon him. 'What do you mean, what am *I* going to do? I'm a prisoner here, too. When they had the big roundup, I got snatched away from a wife and three kids, the same as you got pulled away from your used car lot. What the hell do you want me to do? Beg them not to bash their heads against the lucite, it'll smear our nice north view of space!'

Samswope wiped both hands across his faces simultaneously in a weary pattern. The blue eyes of his left head closed, and the brown eyes of his right head blinked quickly. His left head, which had been speaking till now, nodded onto his chest. His right head, the nearly-dumb one, mumbled incoherently—Samswope's left head jerked up, and a look of disgust and hatred clouded his eyes. 'Shut up, you—fucking moron!' He cracked his right head with a full fist.

Bedzyk watched without pity. The first time he had seen Samswope flail himself—would flagellate be a better term?—he had pitied the mutant. But it was a constant thing now, the way Samswope took his agony out on the dumb head. And there were times Bedzyk thought Samswope was better off than most. At least he had a release valve, an object of hate.

'Take it easy, Sam. Nothing's going to help us, not a single, lousy th——'

Samswope snapped a look at Bedzyk, then catalogued the thick arms and huge chest of the man, and wearily murmured: 'Oh, I don't know, Bedzyk, I don't know.' He dropped his left head into his hands. The right one winked imbecilically at Bedzyk. Bedzyk shuddered and looked away.

'If only we could have made that landing on Venus,' Samswope intoned from the depths of his hands. 'If only they'd let us in.'

'You ought to know by now, Sam,' Bedzyk reminded him bitterly, 'there's no room for us in the System at all. No room on Earth and nowhere else. They've got allocations and quotas and assignments. So many to Io, so many to Callisto, so many to Luna and Venus and Mars and anyplace else you might want to settle down. No room for Discards. No room in space, at all.'

Across the saloon three fish-men, their heads encased in bubbling clear helmets, had gotten into a squabble, and two of them were trying to open the petcock on the third's helmet. This was something else again; the third fish-man was struggling, he didn't want to die gasping. This was not a suicide, but a murder, if they let it go unchecked.

Bedzyk leaped to his feet and hurled himself at the two attacking fish-men. He caught one by the bicep and spun him. His fist was half-cocked before he realized one solid blow would shatter the water-globe surrounding the fish-face, would kill the mutant. Instead, he took him around and shoved him solidly by the back of the shoulders, toward the compartment door. The fish-man stumbled away, breathing bubbly imprecations into his life water, casting furious glances back at his companions. The second fish-man came away of his own accord and followed the first from the saloon.

Bedzyk helped the last fish-man to a relaxer and watched disinterestedly as the mutant let a fresh supply of air bubbles into the circulating water in the globe. The fish-man mouthed a lipless thanks, and Bedzyk passed it away with a gesture. He went back to his seat.

Samswope was massaging the dumb head. 'Those three'll never grow up.'

Bedzyk fell into the chair. 'You wouldn't be too happy living inside a goldfish bowl yourself, Swope.'

Samswope stopped massaging the wrinkled yellow skin of the dumb head, seemed prepared to snap a retort, but a blip and clear-squawk from the intercom stopped him.

'Bedzyk! Bedzyk, you down there?' It was the voice of Harmony Teat up in the drive room. Why was it they always called *him*? Why did they persist in making him their arbiter?

'Yeah, I'm here, in the saloon. What's up?'

The squawk-box blipped again and Harmony Teat's mellow voice came to him from the ceiling. 'I just registered a ship coming in on us, off about three-thirty. I checked through the ephemeris and the shipping schedules. Nothing supposed to be out there. What should I do? You think it's a customs ship from Earth?'

Bedzyk heaved himself to his feet. He sighed. 'No, I don't think it's a customs ship. They threw us out, but I doubt if they have the imagination or gall to extract tithe from us for being here. I don't know what it might be, Harmony. Hold everything and record any signals they send. I'm on my way upship.'

He strode quickly out of the saloon, and up the cross-leveled ramps toward the drive room. Not till he had passed the hydroponics level did he realize Samswope was behind him. 'I, uh, thought I'd come along, Bed,' Samswope said apologetically, wringing his small, red hands. 'I didn't want to stay down there with those—those freaks.'

His dumb head hung off to one side, sleeping fitfully.

Bedzyk did not answer. He turned on his heel and casually strode updecks, not looking back.

There was no trouble. The ship identified itself when it was well away. It was an Attaché Carrier from System Central in Butte, Montana, Earth. The supercargo was a SpecAttaché named Curran. When the ship pulled alongside the Discard vessel and jockeyed for grappling position, Harmony Teat (her long gray-green hair reaching down past the spiked projections on her spinal column) threw on the *attract* field for that section of the hull. The Earth ship clunked against the Discard vessel, and the locks were synched in.

Curran came across without a suit.

He was a slim, incredibly tanned young man with a crewcut clipped so short, a patch of nearly-bald showed at the center of his scalp. His eyes were alert, and his manner was brisk and friendly, that of the professional dignitary in the Foreign Service.

Bedzyk did not bother with amenities.

'What do you want?'

'Who may I be addressing, sir, if I may ask?' Curran was the perfect model of diplomacy.

'Bedzyk is what I was called on Earth.' Cool, disdainful, I-may-he-hideous-but-I-still-have-a-little-pride.

'My name is Curran, Mr. Curran, Mr. Bedzyk. Alan Curran of System Central. I've been asked to come out and speak to you about——'

Bedzyk settled against the bulkhead opposite the lock, not even offering the Attaché an invitation to return to the saloon.

'You want us to get out of your sky, is that it? You stinking lousy ...' He faltered in fury. He could not finish the sentence, so steeped in anger was he. 'You set off too many bombs down there, and eventually some of us with something in our bloodstreams react to it, and we turn into monsters. What do you do ... you call it the Sickness and you pack us up whether we want to go or not, and you shove us into space.'

'Mr. Bedzyk, I——'

'You *what*? You damned well *what*, Mr. System Central? With your straight, clean body and your nice home on Earth, and your allocations of how many people live where to keep the balance of culture just so! You *what*? You want to invite us to leave? Okay, we'll go,' he was nearly screeching, his face crimson with emotion, his big hands knotted at his sides in fear he would strike this emissary.

'We'll get out of your sky. We've been all the way out to the Edge, Mr. Curran, and there's no room in space for us anywhere. They won't let us land even on the frontier worlds where we can pay our way. Oh no, contamination, they think. Okay, don't shove, Curran, we'll be going.'

He started to turn away, was nearly down the passageway, when Curran's solid voice stopped him: 'Bedzyk!'

The wedge-chested man turned. Curran was unsticking the seam that sealed his jumper top. He pulled it open and revealed his chest.

It was covered with leprous green and brown sores. His face was a blasted thing, then. He was a man with Sickness, who wanted to know how he had acquired it—how he could be rid of it. On the ship, they called Curran's particular deformity 'the runnies.'

Bedzyk walked back slowly, his eyes never leaving

Curran's face. 'They sent you to talk to us?' Bedzyk asked, wondering.

Curran resealed the jumper, and nodded. He laid a hand on his chest, as though wishing to be certain the sores would not run off and leave him. A terror swam brightly in his young eyes.

'It's getting worse down there, Bedzyk,' he said as if in a terrible need for hurrying. 'There are more and more changing every day. I've never seen anything like it——'

He hesitated, shuddered.

He ran a hand over his face, and swayed slightly, as though whatever memory he now clutched to himself was about to make him faint. 'I—I'd like to sit down.'

Bedzyk took him by the elbow, and led him a few steps toward the saloon. Then Dresden, the girl with the glass hands—who wore monstrous cotton-filled gloves—came out from the connecting passage leading to the saloon, and Bedzyk thought of the hundred weird forms Curran would have to face. In his condition, that would be bad. He turned the other way, and led Curran back up to the drive room. Bedzyk waved at a control chair. 'Have a seat.'

Curran looked collegiate-boy shook-up. He sank into the chair, again touching his chest in disbelief. 'I've been like this for over two months . . . they haven't found out yet; I've tried to keep myself from showing it . . .'

He was shivering wildly.

Bedzyk perched on the shelf on the plot-tank, and crossed his legs. He folded his arms across his huge chest and looked at Curran. 'What do they want down there? What do they want from their beloved Discards?' He savored the last word with the taste of alum.

'It's, it's so bad you won't believe it, Bedzyk.' He ran a hand through his crewcut, nervously. 'We thought we had the Sickness licked. There was every reason to believe the atmosphere spray Terra Pharmaceuticals developed would end it. They sprayed the entire planet, but something they didn't even know was in the spray, and something they only half-suspected in the Sickness combined, and produced a healthier strain.

'That was when it started getting bad. What had been a hit-and-miss thing—with just a few like yourselves, with some weakness in your bloodstreams making you susceptible—became a rule instead of an exception. People started changing while you watched. I—I' he faltered again, shuddered at a memory.

'My, my fiancée,' he went on, looking at his attaché case and his hands, 'I was eating lunch with her in Rockefeller Plaza's Skytop. We had to be back at work in Butte in twenty minutes, just time to catch a cab, and she—she—*changed* while we were sitting there. Her eyes, they, they—I can't explain it, you can't know what it was like seeing them water and run down her ch-cheeks like that, it was——' his face tightened up as though he were trying to keep himself from going completely insane.

Bedzyk sharply curbed the hysteria. 'We have seven people like that on board right now. I know what you mean. And they aren't the worst. Go on, you were saying?'

Such prosaic acceptance of the horror brought Curran's frenzy down. 'It got so bad everyone was staying in the sterile shelters. The streets always empty; it was horrible. Then some quack physician out in Cincinnati or somewhere like that came up with an answer. A serum made from a secretion in the bloodstreams of—of——'

Bedzyk added the last word for him: 'Of Discards?'

Curran nodded soberly.

Bedzyk's hard-edged laugh rattled against Curran's thin film of calm. He jerked his eyes to the man sitting on the plot-tank. A furious expression came over him.

'What are you laughing at? We need your help! We

need all you people as blood donors.'

Bedzyk stopped laughing abruptly. 'Why not use the changed ones from down there.' He jerked a thumb at the big lucite viewport where Earth hung swollen and multicolored. 'What's wrong with them——' and he added with malice '—with you?' Curran twitched as he realized he could so easily be lumped in with the afflicted.

'We're no good. We were changed by this new mutated Sickness. The secretion is different in our blood than it is in yours. You were stricken by the primary Sickness, or virus, or whatever they call it. We have a complicated one. But the way the research has outlined it, the only ones who have what we need, are you Dis——' he caught himself '—you people who were shipped out before the Sickness itself mutated.'

Bedzyk snorted contemptuously. He let a wry, astonished smirk tickle his lips. "You Earthies are fantastic.' He shook his head in private amusement.

He slipped off the plot-tank's ledge and turned to the port, talking half to himself, half to a nonexistent third person in the drive room. 'These Earthies are unbelievable! Can you imagine, can you *picture* it?' Astonishment rang in his disbelief at the proposal. 'First they hustle us into a metal prison and shoot us out here to die alone, they don't want any part of us, go away they say. Then when the trouble comes to them too big, they run after us, can you help us please, you dirty, ugly things, help us nice clean Earthies.' He spun suddenly. 'Get out of here! Get off this ship! We won't help you.

'You have your allotments and your quotas for each world——'

Curran broke in, 'Yes, that's it. If the population goes down much more, they've been killing themselves, riots, it's terrible, then the balance will be changed, and our entire System culture will bend and fall and——'

Bedzyk cut him off, finishing what he had been saying, '—yes, you have your dirty little quotas, but you have no room for us. Well, we've got no room for you! Now get the hell off this ship. We don't want to help you!'

Curran leaped to his feet. 'You can't send me away like this! You don't speak for all of them aboard. You can't treat a Terran emissary this way——' Bedzyk had him by the jumper, and had propelled him toward the closed companionway door before the Attaché knew quite what was happening. He hit the door and rebounded. As he stumbled back toward Bedzyk, the great-chested mutant snatched the briefcase from beside the control chair and slammed it into Curran's stomach. 'Here! Here's your offer and your lousy demands, and get off this ship! We don't want any part of y——'

The door crashed open, and the Discards were there.

They filled the corridor, as far back as the angle where cross-passages ran off toward the saloon and galley. They shoved and nudged each other to get a view into the drive room; Samswope and Harmony Teat and Dresden were in the front, and from somewhere Samswope had produced an effectively deadly little rasp-pistol. He held it tightly, threateningly, and Bedzyk felt flattered that they had come to his aid.

'You don't need that, Sam—Mr. Curran was just leav——'

Then he realized. The rasp was pointed not at Curran, but at him.

He stood frozen, one hand still clutching Curran's sleeve, as Curran bellied the briefcase to himself.

'Dresden overheard it all, Mr. Curran,' Samswope said in a pathetically ingratiating tone. '*He* wants us to rot on this barge.' He gestured at Bedzyk with his free hand as the dumb head nodded certain agreement. 'What offer can you make us, can we go home, Mr. Curran . . .?'

There was a whimpering and a pleading in Samswope's voice that Bedzyk had only *sensed* before.

He tried to break in, 'Are you insane, Swope? Putty, that's all you are! Putty when you see a fake hope that you'll get off this ship! Can't you see they just want to *use* us? Can't you understand that?'

Samswope's face grew livid and he screamed, 'Shut up! Just shut up and let Curran talk! We don't want to die on this ship. *You* may like it, you little tin god, but we hate it here! So shut up and let him talk!'

Curran spoke rapidly then: 'If you allow us to send a medical detachment up here to use you as blood donors, I have the word of the System Central that you will all be allowed to land on Earth and we'll have a reservation for you so you can live some kind of normal lives again——'

'Hey, what's the matter with you?' Bedzyk again burst in, trying vainly to speak over the hubbub from the corridor. 'Can't you see he's lying? They'll use us and then desert us again!'

Samswope growled menacingly, 'If you don't shut up I'll kill you, Bedzyk!'

Bedzyk faltered into silence and watched the scene before him. They were melting. They were going to let this rotten turncoat Earthie blind them with false hopes.

'We've worked our allotments around so there is space for you, perhaps in the new green-valleys of South America or on the veldtland in Rhodesia. It will be wonderful, but we need your blood, we need your help.'

'Don't trust him! Don't believe him, you can't believe an Earthman!' Bedzyk shouted, stumbling forward to wrest the rasp-pistol from Samswope's grip.

Samswope fired point-blank. First the rasp of the power spurting from the muzzle of the tiny pistol filled the drive room, then the smell of burning flesh, and Bedzyk's eyes opened wide in pain. He screamed thinly, and staggered back against Curran. Curran stepped aside, and Bedzyk mewed in agony, and crumpled onto the deck. A huge hole had been seared through his huge chest. Huge chest, huge death, and he lay there with his eyes open, barely forming the words 'Don't . . . you can't, can't t-trust an Earth-mmm . . .' with his bloody lips. The last word formed and became a forever intaglio.

Curran's face had paled out till it was a blotch against the dark blue of his jumper. 'Y-y-y . . .'

Samswope moved into the drive room and took Curran by the sleeve, almost where Bedzyk had held it. 'You promise us we can land and be allowed to settle someplace on Earth?'

Curran nodded dumbly. Had they asked for Earth in its socket, he would have nodded agreement. Samswope still held the rasp.

'All right, then . . . get your med detachment up here, and get that blood. We want to go home, Mr. Curran, we want to go home more than anything!'

They led him to the lock. Behind him, Curran saw three mutants lifting the blasted body of Bedzyk, bearing it on their shoulders through the crowd. The body was borne out of sight down a cross-corridor, and Curran followed it out of sight with his eyes.

Beside him, Samswope said: 'To the garbage lock. We go that way, Mr. Curran.' His tones were hard and uncompromising. 'We don't like going that way, Mr. Curran. We want to go home. You'll see to it, won't you, Mr. Curran?'

Curran again nodded dumbly, and entered the lock linking ships.

Ten hours later, the med detachment came up. The Discards were completely obedient and tremendously helpful.

It took nearly eleven months to inoculate the entire population of the Earth and the rest of the System—strictly as preventive caution dictated—and during that time no more Discards took their lives. Why should they? They were going home. Soon the tug-ships would come, and help jockey the big Discard vessel into orbit for the run to Earth. They were going home. There was room for them now, even in their condition. Spirits ran high, and laughter tinkled oddly down the passageway in the 'evenings.' There was even a wedding between Arkay (who was blind and had a bushy tail) and a pretty young thing the others called Daanae, for she could not speak herself. Without a mouth that was impossible. At the ceremony in the saloon, Samswope acted as minister, for the Discards had made him their leader, in the same, silent way they had made Bedzyk the leader before him. Spirits ran high, and the constant knowledge that as soon as Earth had the Sickness under control, they would be going home.

Then one 'afternoon' the ship came.

Not the little tugs, as they had supposed, but a cargo ship nearly as big as their own home. Samswope rushed to synch in the locks, and when the red lights merged on the board, he locked the two together firmly, and scrambled back through the throng to be the first to greet the men who would deliver them.

When the lock sighed open, and they saw the first ten who had been thrust in, they knew the truth.

One had a head flat as a plate, with no eyes, and its mouth in its neck. Another had several hundred thousand slimy tentacles where arms should have been, and waddled on stumps that could never again be legs. Still another was brought in by a pair of huge empty-faced men, in a bowl. The bowl contained a yellow jelly, and swimming in the yellow jelly was the woman.

Then they knew. They were not going home. As lockful after lockful of more Discards came through, to swell their ranks even more, they knew these were the last of the tainted ones from Earth. The last ones who had been stricken by the Sickness—who had changed before the serum could save them. These were the last, and now the Earth was clean.

Samswope watched them trail in, some dragging themselves on appendageless torsos, others in baskets, still others with one arm growing from a chest, or hair that was blue and fungus growing out all over the body. He watched them and knew the man he had killed had been correct. For among the crowd he glimpsed a bare-chested Discard with huge sores on his body. Curran.

And as the cargo ship unlocked and swept back to Earth—with the silent warning *Don't follow us, don't try to land, there's no room for you here*— Samswope could hear Bedzyk's hysterical tones in his head:

Don't trust them! There no room for us anywhere! Don't trust them!

You can't trust an Earthman!

Samswope started walking slowly toward the galley, knowing he would need someone to seal the garbage lock after him. But it didn't matter who it was. There were more than enough Discards aboard now.

Deeper Than the Darkness

They came to Alf Gunnderson in the Pawnee County jail.

He was sitting against the plasteel wall of the cell, hugging his bony knees. On the plasteel floor lay an ancient, three-string mandolin he had borrowed from the deputy and had been plunking with some talent off and on all that hot summer day. Under his thick buttocks the empty trough of the mattressless bunk bowed beneath his weight. He was an extremely tall man, even hunched up that way.

He was a gaunt, empty-looking man. His hair fell lanky and drab and gray-brown in disarray over a low forehead. His eyes seemed to be peas, withdrawn from their pods and placed in a starkly white face.

Their blankness only accented the total cipher he seemed. There was no inch of expression or recognition on his face or in the line of his body. He seemed to be a man who had given up the Search long ago.

He was more than tired-looking, more than weary. His was an internal weariness. His face did not change its hollow stare at the plasteel-barred door opposite, even as it swung back to admit the two nonenties.

The two men entered, their stride as alike as the unobtrusive gray mesh suits they wore, as alike as the faces that would fade from memory moments after they had exited. The turnkey—a grizzled country deputy with a minus 8 rating—stared after the men with open wonder on his bearded face.

One of the gray-suited men turned, pinning the wondering stare to the deputy's face. His voice was calm and unrippled. 'Close the door and go back to your desk.' The words were cold and paced. They brooked no opposition. It was obvious: the men were Mindees.

The roar of a late afternoon inverspace ship split the waiting moment, outside; then the turnkey slammed the door, palming its loktite. He walked back out of the cell block, hands deep in his coverall pockets. His head was lowered as though he was trying to solve a complex problem. It, too, was obvious: he was trying to block his thoughts off from those goddamned Mindees.

When he was gone, the telepaths circled Gunnderson slowly. Their faces altered, softly, subtly, and personality flowed in. They shot each other confused glances.

Him? the first man thought, nodding slightly at the still, knee-hugging prisoner.

That's what the report said, Ralph. The other man removed his forehead-concealing snap-brim and sat down on the edge of the bunk-trough. He touched Gunnderson's leg with tentative fingers. *He's not thinking, for God's sake!* the thought flashed. *I can't get a thing.*

Shock sparkled in the thought.

He must be blocked off by trauma-barrier, came the reply from the telepath named Ralph.

'Is your name Alf Gunnderson?' the first Mindee inquired softly, a hand on Gunnderson's shoulder.

The expression never changed. The head swivelled slowly and the dead eyes came to bear on the dark-suited telepath. 'I'm Gunnderson.' His tones indicated no enthusiasm, no curiosity.

The first man looked up at his partner, doubt wrinkling his eyes, pursing his lips. He shrugged his shoulders, as if to say, *Who knows?*

He turned back to Gunnderson.

Immobile, as before. Hewn from rock, silent as the pit.

'What are you in here for, Gunnderson?' He spoke the halting speech of the telepath, as though he was unused to words.

The dead stare swung back to the plasteel bars. 'I set the woods on fire,' he said.

The Mindee's face darkened at the prisoner's words. That was what the report had said. The report that had come in from this remote corner of this remote country.

The American Union covered two continents with plasteel and printed circuits, relays and rapid movement, but there were areas of backwoods country that had never taken to civilizing. They still maintained roads and jails, fishing holes and forests. Out of one of these had come three reports, spaced an hour apart, with startling ramifications—if true. They had been snapped through the primary message banks in Capital City in Buenos Aires, reeled through the computers, and handed to the Bureau for checking. While the inverspace ships plied between worlds, while Earth fought its transgalactic wars, in a rural section of the American continents, a strange thing was happening.

A mile and a half of raging forest fire, and Alf Gunnderson the one responsible. So the Bureau had sent two Mindees.

'How did it start, Alf?'

The dead eyes closed momentarily in pain, then opened, and he answered, 'I was trying to get the pot to heat up. Trying to set the kindling under it to burning. I fired myself too hard.' A flash of self-pity and unbearable hurt came into his face, disappeared just as quickly. Empty once more, he added, 'I always do.'

The first man exhaled sharply, got up and put on his

hat. The personality flowed out of his face. He was a carbon-copy of the other telepath once more. They were no longer individuals; they were Bureau men, studiedly, exactly, precisely alike in every detail.

'This is the one,' he said.

'Come on, Alf,' the Mindee named Ralph said. 'Let's go.'

The authority in his voice no more served to move Gunnderson than their initial appearance had. He sat as he was. The two men looked at one another.

What's the matter with him? the second one flashed.

If you had what he's got—you'd be a bit buggy yourself, the first one replied.

They hoisted the prisoner under his arms, lifted him, unresisting, off the bunk. The turnkey came at a call, and—still marveling at these men who had come in, shown Bureau cards, sworn him to deadly silence, and were now taking the tramp firebug with them—opened the cell door.

As they passed before him, the telepath named Ralph turned suddenly sharp and piercing eyes on the old guard. 'This is government business, mister,' he warned. 'One word of this, and you'll be a prisoner in your own jail. Digit?'

The turnkey bobbed his head quickly.

'And stop thinking, mister,' the Mindee added nastily, 'we don't like to be referred to as slimy peekers!' The turnkey turned a shade paler and watched silently as they disappeared down the hall, out of the Pawnee County jailhouse. He waited, blanking fiercely, till he heard the whine of the Bureau solocab rising into the afternoon sky.

Now what the devil did they want with a crazy firebug hobo like that? He thought viciously, *goddam Mindees!*

After they had flown him to Buenos Aires, deep in the

heart of the blasted Argentine desert, they sent him in for testing.

The testing was exhaustive. Even though he did not really cooperate, there were things he could not keep them from learning, things that showed up because they were there:

Such as his ability to start fires with his mind.

Such as the fact that he could not control the blazes.

Such as the fact that he had been bumming for fifteen years in an effort to find peace and seclusion.

Such as the fact that he had become a tortured and unhappy man because of his strange mind-power...

'Alf,' said the bodiless voice from the rear of the darkened auditorium, 'light that cigarette on the table. Put it in your mouth and make it light, Alf. Without a match.'

Alf Gunnderson stood in the circle of light. He shifted from leg to leg on the blazing stage, and eyed the cylinder of white paper on the table.

He was trapped in it again. The harrying, the testing, the staring. He was different—even from the other accredited psioid types—and they would try to put him away. It had happened before, it was happening now. There was no real peace for him.

'I don't smoke,' he said, which was not true. But this scene was brother to the uncountable police lineups he had gone through, all the way across the American continents, across Earth, to A Centauri IX and back. It annoyed him, and it terrified him, for he knew he could not escape.

Except this time there were no hard rocky-faced cops out there in the darkness beyond his sight. This time there were hard, rocky-faced Bureau men and SpaceCom officials.

Even Terrence, head of SpaceCom, was sitting in one of those pneumoseats, watching him steadily.

Daring him to be what he was!

He lifted the cylinder hesitantly, almost put it back. 'Smoke it, Alf!' snapped a different voice, deeper in tone, from the darkness.

He put the cigarette between his lips. The men waited.

He wanted to say something, perhaps to object, but he could not. Alf Gunnderson's heavy brows drew down. His blank eyes became—if it were possible—even blanker. A sharp, denting V appeared between the brows.

The cigarette flamed into life.

A tongue of fire leaped up from the tip. In an instant it had consumed tobacco, paper, and denicotizer in one roar. The fire slammed against Gunnderson's lips, searing them, lapping at his nose, his face.

He screamed, fell on his face and beat at the flames with his hands.

Suddenly the stage was clogged with running men in the blue and charcoal suits of the SpaceCom. Gunnderson lay writhing on the floor, a wisp of charry smoke rising from his face. One of the SpaceCom officials broke the cap on an extinguisher vial and the spray washed over the body of the fallen man.

'Get the Mallaport! Get the goddamned Mallaport, willya!' A young ensign with brush-cut blond hair, first to reach the stage, as though he had been waiting crouched below, cradled Gunnderson's head in his muscular arms, brushing with horror at the flakes of charred skin. He had the watery blue eyes of the spaceman, the man who has seen terrible things; yet his eyes were more frightened now than any man's eyes had a right to be.

In a few minutes the angular, spade-jawed, Malleable-Transporter was smoothing the skin on Gunnderson's face, realigning the atoms—shearing away the burned flesh, coating it with vibrant, healthy pink skin.

Another few moments and the psioid was finished. The burns had been erased; Gunnderson was new and whole, save for the patches of healthier-seeming skin that dotted his face.

All through it he had been murmuring. As the Mallaport finished his mental work and stood up with a sigh, the words filtered through to the young SpaceCom ensign. He stared at Gunnderson a moment, then raised his watery blue eyes to the other officials standing about.

He stared at them with a mixture of fear and bewilderment.

Gunnderson had been saying: 'Let me die, please let me die, I want to die, won't you let me die, please...'

Chapter Two

The ship was heading toward Omalo, sun of the Delgart system. It had been translated into inverspace by a Driver named Carina Correia. She had warped the ship through, and gone back to her deep-sleep, till she was needed at Omalo snap-out.

Now the ship whirled through the crazy quilt of inverspace, cutting through to the star system of Earth's adversary.

Gunnderson sat in the cabin with the brush-cut blond ensign. All through the trip, since blast-off and snap-out, the Pyrotic had been kept in his stateroom. This was the newest of the Earth SpaceCom ships, yet he had seen none of it. Just this tiny stateroom, and the constant company of the ensign.

The SpaceCom ensign's watery blue eyes swept between the pallid man and the teleport-proof safe set in the cabin's bulkhead.

'Any idea why they're sending us so deep into Delgart territory?' the ensign fished. 'It's pretty tight lines up this far. Must be something big. Any idea?'

Gunnderson's eyes came up from their focus on his boot-tops, and stared at the spaceman. He idly flipped the harmonica he had requested before blast-off and had used to pass away the long hours in inverspace. 'No idea. How long have we been at war with the Delgarts?'

'Don't you even know who your planet's at war with?'

'I've been rural for many years. And aren't we *always* at war with someone?'

The ensign looked startled. 'Not unless it's to protect the peace of the galaxies. Earth is a peace-loving——'

Gunnderson cut him off. 'Yes. I know. But how long have we been at war with the Delgarts? I thought they were our allies under some treaty or other?'

The spaceman's face contorted in a picture of conditioned hatred. 'We've been after the bastards since they jumped one of our mining planets outside their cluster.' He twisted his lips in open loathing. 'We'll clean the bastards out soon enough! Teach *them* to jump peaceful Earthmen.'

Gunnderson wished he could shut out the words. He had heard the same story all the way to A Centauri IX and back. Someone had always jumped someone else; someone was always at war with someone else; there were always bastards to be cleaned out...

The invership whipped past the myriad colors of inverspace, hurtling through that not-space toward the alien cluster. Gunnderson sat in the teleport-proof stateroom, triple-loktited, and waited. He had no idea what they wanted of him, why they had tested him, why they had sent him through the preflight checkups, why he was here. But he knew one thing: whatever it was, there was to be no peace for *him* . . . ever.

He silently cursed the strange mental power he had. The power to make the molecules of *anything* speed up tremendously, making them grind against one another, causing combustion. A strange, channeled teleport faculty that was useless for anything but the creation of fire. He damned it soulfully, wishing he had been born deaf, mute, blind, incapable of any contact with the world.

From the moment of his life when he had become aware of his strange power, he had been haunted. No control, no identification, no communication. Cut off. Tagged as an oddie. Not even the pleasures of being an acknowledged psioid like the Mindees, the invaluable Drivers, the Blasters, or the Mallaports who could move the atoms of flesh to their design. He was an oddie: a nondirective psioid. Tagged deadly and uncontrollable. He could set the fires, but he could not control them. The molecules were too tiny, too quickly imitative for him to stop the activity once it started. It had to stop of its own volition—and usually it was too long in stopping.

Once he had thought himself normal, once he had thought of leading an ordinary life—of perhaps becoming a musician. But that idea had died aflaming, as all other normal ideas had followed it.

First the ostracism, then the hunting, then the arrests and the prison terms, one after another. Now something new—something he could not understand. What did they want with him? It was obviously in connection with the mighty battle being fought between Earth and the Delgarts, but of what use could his unreliable powers be?

Why was he in this most marvelous of the new Space-Com ships, heading toward the central sun of the enemy cluster? And why should he help Earth in any case?

At that moment the locks popped, the safe broke open, and the clanging of the alarms was heard to the bowels of the inversship.

The ensign stopped him as he rose and started toward the safe. The ensign thumbed a button on his wrist-console.

'Hold it, Mr. Gunnderson. I wasn't told what was in there, but I was told to keep you away from it until the other two get here.'

Gunnderson slumped back hopelessly on the acceleration-bunk. He dropped the harmonica to the metal floor and lowered his head into his hands. 'What other two?'

'I don't know, sir. I wasn't told.'

The other two were psioids, naturally.

When the Mindee and the Blaster arrived, they motioned the ensign to remove the contents of the safe. He walked over nervously, took out the tiny recorder and the single speak-tip.

'Play it, Ensign,' the Mindee directed.

The spaceman thumbed the speak-tip into the hole, and the grating of the blank space at the beginning of the record filled the room.

'You can leave now, Ensign,' the Mindee said.

After the SpaceCom officer had securely loktited the door, the voice began. Gunnderson recognized it immediately as that of Terrence, head of SpaceCom. The man who had questioned him tirelessly at the Bureau building in Buenos Aires. Terrence: hero of another war, the Earth-Kyben War, now head of SpaceCom. The words were brittle, almost without inflection, yet they carried a sense of utmost importance:

'Gunnderson,' he began, 'We have, as you already know, a job for you. By this time the ship will have reached the central-point of your trip through inverspace.

'You will arrive in two days Earthtime at a slip-out point approximately five million miles from Omalo, the enemy sun. You will be far behind enemy lines, but we are certain you will be able to accomplish your mission safely. That is why you have been given this new ship. It can withstand anything the enemy can throw.

'We want you to get back after your job is done. You are the most important man in our war effort, Gunnderson, and this is only your first mission.

'We want you to turn the sun Omalo into a supernova.'

Gunnderson, for perhaps the second time in thirty-eight years of bleak, gray life, was staggered. The very concept made his stomach churn. Turn another race's sun into a flaming, gaseous bomb of incalculable power, spreading death into space, charring into nothing the planets of the system? Annihilate in one move an entire culture?

What did they think he was capable of?

Could he direct his mind to such a task?

Could he do it?

Should he do it?

His mind trembled at the possibility. He had never really considered himself as having many ideals. He had set fires in warehouses to get the owners their liability insurance; he had flamed other hobos who had tried to rob him; he had used the unpredictable power of his mind for many things, but this——

This was the murder of a solar system!

He wasn't in any way sure he *could* turn a sun supernova. What was there to lead them to think he might be able to do it? Burning a forest and burning a giant red sun were two things fantastically far apart. It was something out of a nightmare. But even if he *could*...

'In case you find the task unpleasant, Mr. Gunnderson,' the ice-chip voice of the SpaceCom head continued, 'we have included in this ship's complement a Mindee and a Blaster.

'Their sole job is to watch and protect you, Mr. Gunnderson. To make certain you are kept in the proper, *patriotic* state of mind. They have been instructed to read you from this moment on, and should you not be willing to carry out your assignment . . . well, I'm certain you are familiar with a Blaster's capabilities.'

Gunnderson stared at the blank-faced telepath sitting across from him on the other bunk. The man was obviously listening to every thought in Gunnderson's head. A strange, nervous expression was on the Mindee's face. His gaze turned to the Blaster who accompanied him, then back to Gunnderson.

The Pyrotic swiveled a glance at the Blaster, then swiveled away as quickly.

Blasters were men meant to do one job, one job only; a Blaster became the type of man he *had* to be, to be successful doing that job. They all looked the same, and now Gunnderson found the look almost terrifying. He had not thought he could *be* terrified, any more.

'That is your assignment, Gunnderson, and if you have any hesitation, remember our enemy is *not* human. They may look like you, but mentally they are extraterrestrials as unlike you as you are unlike a slug. And remember there's a war on. You will be saving the lives of many Earthmen by performing this task.

'This is your chance to become respected, Gunnderson.

'A hero, respected, and for the first time,' he paused, as though not wishing to say what was next, 'for the first time—worthy of your world.'

The rasp-rasp-rasp of the speak-tip filled the stateroom. Gunnderson said nothing. He could hear the phrase whirling, whirling in his head: There's a war on, *There's a war on,* THERE'S A WAR ON! He stood up and slowly walked to the door.

'Sorry, Mr. Gunnderson,' the Mindee said emphatically, 'we can't allow you to leave this room.'

He sat down and lifted the battered mouth organ from

where it had fallen. He fingered it for a while, then put it to his lips. He blew, but made no sound.

And he didn't leave.

Chapter Three

They thought he was asleep. The Mindee—a cadaverously thin man with hair grayed at the temples and slicked back in strips on top, with a gasping speech and a nervous movement of hand to ear—spoke to the Blaster.

'He doesn't seem to be thinking, John!'

The Blaster's smooth, hard features moved vaguely, and a quirking frown split his inkline mouth. 'Can he do it?'

The Mindee rose, ran a hand quickly through the straight, slicked hair.

'Can he do it? No, he shouldn't be *able* to do it, but he's doing it! I can't figure it out . . . it's eerie. Either I've lost it, or he's got something new.'

'Trauma-barrier?'

'That's what they told me before I left, that he seemed to be blocked off. But they thought it was only temporary, and that once he was away from the Bureau buildings he'd clear up.'

'But he *hasn't* cleared up.'

The Blaster looked concerned. 'Maybe it's you.'

'I didn't get a Master's rating for nothing, John, and I tell you there isn't a trauma-barrier I can't at least get *something* through. If only a snatch of gabble. But here there's nothing—nothing!'

'Maybe it's you,' the Blaster repeated, still concerned.

'Damn it! It's *not* me! I can read you, can't I—your right foot hurts from new boots, you wish you could have the bunk to lie down on, you ... Oh, hell, I can read *you*, and I can read the Captain up front, and I can read the pitmen in the hold, but I *can't* read *him*!

'It's like hitting a sheet of glass in his head. There should be a reflection if not penetration, but he seems to be opaqued. I didn't want to say anything when he was awake, of course.'

'Do you think I should twit him a little—wake him up and warn him we're on to his game?'

The Mindee raised a hand to stop the very thought of the Blaster. 'Great Gods, no!' He gestured wildly. 'This Gunnderson's invaluable. If they found out we'd done anything unauthorized to him, we'd both be tanked.'

Gunnderson lay on his acceleration-bunk, feigning sleep, listening to them. It was a new discovery to him, what they were saying. He had sometimes suspected that the pyrotic faculty of his mind was not the only way he differed from the norm—perhaps there were others. And if it was a side-effect, there *ought* to be others. He knew *he* could not read minds; was this impenetrability by Mindees another factor?

Perhaps the Blaster was powerless against him, too.

It would never clear away his problem—that was something he could do only in his own mind—but it might make his position and final decision safer.

There was only one way to find out. He knew the Blaster could not actually harm him severely, by Space-Com's orders; but he wouldn't hesitate to blast off one of the Pyrotic's arms—cauterizing it as it disappeared—to warn him, if the situation seemed desperate enough.

The Blaster had seemed to Gunnderson a singularly

over-zealous man, in any case. It was a terrible risk, but he had to know.

There was only one way to find out, and he took it, finding a startling new vitality in himself for the first time in over thirty years.

He snapped his legs off the bunk, and lunged across the stateroom, shouldering aside the Mindee and straight-arming the Blaster in the mouth. The Blaster, surprised by the rapid and completely unexpected movement, had a reflex thought, and one entire bulkhead was washed by bolts of power. They crackled, and the plasteel buckled. His direction had been upset, but Gunnderson knew the instant he regained his mental balance, the power would be directed at him.

Gunnderson was at the stateroom door, palming the loktite open—having watched the manner used by the Blaster when he had left on several occasions—and putting one foot into the companionway.

Then the Blaster struck. His fury rose, and he lost his sense of duty. This man had struck him—an accepted psioid, not an oddie! The black of his eyes deepened, and his face strained. His cheekbones rose in the stricture of a grin, and the *force* materialized.

It was all around Gunnderson.

He could feel the heat . . . see his clothes sparking and disappearing . . . feel his hair charring at the tips . . . feel the strain of psi power in the air.

But there was no effect on *him*.

He was safe—safe from the power of the Blaster.

Then he knew he didn't have to run, and he turned back to the cabin.

The two psioids were staring at him in open terror.

It was almost always night in inverspace.

The ship ploughed constantly through a swamp of black, with metal inside, and metal outside, and the cold unchanging devil-dark beyond the metal. Men hated inverspace—they sometimes took the years-long journey through normal space, to avoid the chilling mystery of inverspace. For one moment the total black would surround the ship, and the next they would be sifting through a field of changing, flickering crazy quilt colors. Then dark again, then light, then dots, then shafts, then the dark once more. It was ever-changing, like a madman's dream. But not interestingly changing, so one would wish to watch, as one might watch a kaleidoscope. This was strange, and unnatural, something beyond the powers of the mind, or the abilities of the eye to comprehend. Ports were unlocked only in the officer's country, and those had solid lead shields that would slam down and dog closed at the slap of a button. Nothing else could be done: for men were men, and space was their eternal enemy. But no man willingly stared back at the deep of inverspace.

In the officer's country, Alf Gunnderson reached with his sight and his mind into the coal-soot that now lay beyond the ship. Since he had proved his invulnerability over the Blaster, he had been given the run of the ship. Where could he go? Nowhere that he could not be found. Guards watched the egress ports at all times, so he was still, in effect, a prisoner on the inversship.

He stared from the giant quartz window, all shields open, all the darkness flowing in. The cabin was dark, but not half so dark as that darkness that was everywhere.

That darkness deeper than the darkness.

What was he? Was he man or was he machine, to be told he must turn a sun nova? What of the people on that sun's planets? What of the women and the children, alien or not? What of the people who hated war, and the people who served because they had been told to serve, and the people who wanted to be left alone? What of the men who went into the fields, while their fellow troops dutifully sharpened their war knives, and cried? Cried because they were afraid, and they were tired, and they wanted home without death. What of those men?

Was this war one of salvation or liberation or duty as they parroted the phrases of patriotism? Or was this still another of the unending wars for domination, larger holdings, richer worlds? Was this another vast joke of the Universe, where men were sent to their deaths so one type of government, no better than another, could rule? He didn't know. He wasn't sure. He was afraid. He had a power beyond all powers in his hands, and he suddenly found himself not a tramp and a waste, but a man who might demolish a solar system at his own will.

Not even sure he *could* do it, he considered the possibility, and it terrified him, making his legs turn to rubber, his blood to liquid oxygen. He was suddenly quite lost, and immersed in a deeper darkness than he had ever known. With no way out.

He spoke to himself, letting his words sound foolish to himself, but speaking them just the same, knowing he had avoided speaking them for far too long:

'Can I do it?

'Should I? I've waited so long, so long, to find a place, and now they tell me I've found a place. Is this my final place? Is this what I've lived and searched for? I can be a valuable war weapon. I can be the man the others turn to when they want a job done. But what sort of job?

'Can I do it? Is it more important to me to find peace —even a peace such as this—and to destroy, than to go on with the unrest?'

Alf Gunnderson stared at the night, at the faint tinges of color beginning to form at the edges of his vision, and his mind washed itself in the water of thought. He had discovered much about himself in the past few days. He had discovered many talents, many ideals he had never suspected in himself.

He had discovered he had character, and that he was not a hopeless, oddie hulk, doomed to die wasted. He found he had a future.

If he could make the proper decision.

But what *was* the proper decision?

'Omalo! Omalo snap-out!'

The cry roared through the companionways, bounced down the halls and against the metal hull of the invership, sprayed from the speakers, and deafened the men asleep beside their squawk-boxes.

The ship ploughed through a maze of colors whose names were unknown, skiiiiittered in a nameless direction, and popped out, shuddering. There it was. The sun of Delgart. Omalo. Big. And golden. With planets set about it like boulders on the edge of the sea. The sea that was space, and from which this ship had come. With death in its hold, and death in its tubes, and death, nothing but death, in its purpose.

The Blaster and the Mindee escorted Alf Gunnderson to the bridge. They stood back and let him walk to the huge quartz portal. The portal before which the Pyrotic had stood so long, so many hours, gazing so deeply into inverspace. They left him there, and stood back, because they knew he was safe from them. No matter how hard they held his arms, no matter how fiercely they pounded thoughts at him, he was safe. He was something new. Not just a Pyrotic, not just a mind-blocked psioid, not just a Blaster-safe, he was something totally new.

Not a composite, for there had been many of those, with imperfect powers of several psi types. But something new, and incomprehensible to his guards. Psioid-plus—with a plus that might mean anything.

Gunnderson moved forward slowly, his deep shadow squirming out before him, sliding up the console, across the portal sill, and across the quartz itself. Himself superimposed across the immensity of space.

The man who was Gunnderson stared into the night that lay without, and at the sun that burned steadily and high in that night. A greater fire raged within him than on that sun.

His was a power he could not even begin to estimate, and if he let it be used in this way, this once, it could be turned to his purpose over and over and over again.

Was there any salvation for him?

'You're supposed to flame that sun, Gunnderson,' the slick-haired Mindee said, trying to assume an authoritative tone, a tone of command, but failing miserably. He knew he was powerless before this man. They could shoot him, of course, but what would that accomplish?

'What are you going to do, Gunnderson? What do you have in mind?' The Blaster chimed in. 'SpaceCom wants Omalo fired. Are you going to do it, or do we have to report you as a traitor?'

'You know what they'll do to you back on Earth, Gunnderson. You know, don't you?'

Alf Gunnderson let the light of Omalo wash his sunken face with red haze. His eyes seemed to deepen in intensity. His hands on the console ledge stiffened and the knuckles turned white. He had seen the possibilities, and he had decided. They would never understand that he had chosen the harder way. He turned slowly.

'Where is the lifescoot located?'

They stared at him, and he repeated his question. They refused to answer, and he shouldered past them, stepped into the droptube to take him below decks. The Mindee spun on him, his face raging.

'You're a coward and a traitor, fireboy! You're a lousy no-psi freak and we'll get you! You can take the lifeboat, but someday we'll find you! No matter where you go out there, we're going to find you!'

He spat then, and the Blaster strained and strained and strained, but the power of his mind had no effect on Gunnderson.

The Pyrotic let the dropshaft lower him, and he found the lifescoot some time later. He took nothing with him but the battered harmonica, and the red flush of Omalo on his face.

When they felt the *pop!* of the lifescoot being snapped into space, and they saw the dark gray dot of it moving away rapidly, flicking quickly off into inverspace, the Blaster and the Mindee slumped into relaxers, stared at each other.

'We'll have to finish the war without him.'

The Blaster nodded. 'He could have won it for us in one minute. And now he's gone.'

'Do you think he could have done it?'

The Blaster shrugged his heavy shoulders.

'He's gone,' the Mindee repeated bitterly. '*He's* gone? Coward! Traitor! Someday ... someday ...'

'Where can he go?'

'He's a wanderer at heart. Space is deep, he can go anywhere.'

'Did you mean that, about finding him someday?'

The Mindee nodded rapidly. 'When they find out, back on Earth, what he did today, they'll start hunting him through all of space. He'll never have another moment's peace. They *have* to find him—he's the perfect weapon. And he can't run forever. They'll find him.'

'A strange man.'

'A man with a power he can't hide, John. We know he can't control it, so how can he hide it? Sooner or later he'll give himself away. He *can't* hide himself cleverly enough to stay hidden forever.'

'Odd that he would turn himself into a fugitive. He could have had peace of mind for the rest of his life. Instead, he's got this ...'

The Mindee stared at the closed portal shields. His tones were bitter and frustrated. 'We'll find him someday.'

The ship shuddered, reversed drives, and slipped back into inverspace.

Chapter Four

Much sky winked back at him.

He sat on the bluff, wind tousling his gray hair, flapping softly at the dirty shirt-tail hanging from his pants top.

The Minstrel sat on the bluff watching the land fall slopingly away under him, down to the shining hide of the sprawling dragon that was a city, lying in the cup of the hills. The dragon that crouched where lush grass had once grown.

On this quiet world, far from a red sun that shone high and steady, the Minstrel sat and pondered the many kinds of peace. And the kind that is not peace, can *never* be peace.

His eyes turned once more to the sage and eternal advice of the blackness above. No one saw him wink back at the silent stars.

With a sigh he slung the battered theremin over his sloping shoulders. It was a portable machine, with both rods bent and its power-pack patched and soldered. His body almost at once assumed the half-slouched, round-shouldered walk of the wanderer. He ambled down the hill toward the rocket field.

They called it the rocket field, out here on the Edge, but they didn't use rockets any longer. Now they rode to space on strange tubes that whistled and sparkled behind the ship till it flicked off into some crazy quilt not-space, and was gone forever.

Tarmac clicked under the heels of his boots. Bright, shining boots, kept meticulously clean by polishing, over-polishing till they reflected back the corona of the field kliegs and, more faintly, the gleam of the stars. The Minstrel kept them cleaned and polished, a clashing note matched against his generally unkempt appearance.

He was tall, towering over almost everyone he had ever met in his homeless wanderings. His body was a lean and supple thing, like a high-tension wire, with the merest suggestion of contained power and quickness. He moved with an easy gait, accentuating his long legs and gangling arms, making his well-proportioned head seem a bubble precariously balanced on a neck too long and thin to support it.

He kept time to the click of the polished boots with a soft half-hum, half whistle. The song was a dead song, long forgotten.

He came from beyond the mountains. No one knew where. No one cared where.

But they listened when he came. They listened almost reverently, with a desperation born of men who know they are severed from their home worlds, who know they will go out and out and seldom come back. He sang of space, and he sang of land, and he sang of the peace that is left for Man—all men, no matter how many arms they had, or what their skin was colored—when he has expended the last little bit of Eternity to which he is entitled.

His voice had the sadness of death in it—the sadness of death before life has finished its work. But it also had the joy of metal under quick fingers, the strength of turned nickel-steel, and the whip of heart and soul working in loneliness. They listened when his song came with the night wind, probing, crying through the darkness of a thousand worlds and on a thousand winds.

The pitmen stopped their work as he came, silent but for the hum of his song and the beat of his boots on the blacktop. They watched as he came across the field.

He had been wandering the star-paths for many years now. He had appeared, and that was all; he was. They knew him as certainly as they knew themselves. They turned and he was like a pillar, set dark against the light and shadow of the field. He paced slowly, and they stopped the hoses feeding the radioactive food to the ships, and the torches with which they flayed the metal skins; and they listened.

The Minstrel knew they were listening, and he unslung his instrument, settling the narrow box with its tone-rods around his neck by its thong. His fingers cajoled and pried and extracted the song of a soul, cast into the pit of the void, left to die, crying in torment not so much at death, but at the terror of being alone when the last call came.

And the workmen cried.

They felt no shame as the tears coursed through the dirt on their faces and mixed with the sweat-shine of their toil. They stood, silent and dreaming, as he came toward them.

And before they even knew it was ended, and for seconds after the wail had fled back across the field into the mountains, they listened to the last notes of his lament.

Hands wiped clumsily across faces, leaving more dirt than before, and backs turned slowly as men resumed work. It seemed they could not face him, the nearer he came; as though he was too deep-seeing, too perceptive for them to be at ease close by. It was a mixture of respect and awe.

The Minstrel stood, waiting.

'Hey! you!'

The Minstrel did not move. There was a pad of soft-soled feet behind him. A spaceman—tanned, supple, almost as tall as the ballad-singer and reminding him of another spaceman, a blond-haired boy he had known long ago—came up beside him.

'What can I do for ya, Minstrel?' asked the spaceman, tones of the accent of a long distant Earth rich in his voice.

'What do they call this world?' the Minstrel asked. His voice was quiet, like a needle being drawn through velvet.

'The natives call it Audi, and the charts call it Rexa Majoris XXIX, Minstrel. Why?'

'It's time to move on.'

The spaceman grinned hugely, lines of amusement crinkling out around his watery brown eyes. 'Need a lift?'

The Minstrel nodded.

The spaceman's face softened, the lines of squinting into the reaches of an eternal night broke and he extended his hand: 'My name's Quantry; top dog on the *Spirit of Lucy Marlowe*. If you don't mind working your way singing for the passengers, we'd be pleased to have you on board.'

The tall man smiled, a quick radiance across the shadows of his face. 'That isn't work.'

'Then done!' exclaimed the spaceman. 'C'mon, I'll fix you a bunk in steerage.'

They walked between the wiper gangs and the pitmen. They threaded their way between the glare of fluorotorches and the sputtering blast of robot welding instruments. The man named Quantry indicated the opening in the smooth side of the ship and the Minstrel clambered inside.

Quantry fixed the berth just behind the reactor feeder-bins, walling off a compartment with an electric blanket draped over a loading track rail. The Minstrel lay on his bunk—a repair bench—with a pillow under his head. He lay thinking.

The moments fled silently and his mind, deep in thought, hardly realized the ports were being dogged home, the radioactive additives being sluiced through their tubes to the converter-cells, the lift tubes being extruded. His mind did not leave its thoughts as the tubes warmed, turning the pit to green glass beneath the ship's bulk. Tubes that would carry the ship to an altitude where the Driver would be wakened from his sleep—or *her* sleep, as was more often the case with that particular breed of psioid—to snap the ship into inverspace.

As the ship came unstuck from solid ground and hurled itself outward on its whistling sparks, the Minstrel lay back, letting the reassuring hand of acceleration press him into deeper reverie. Thoughts spun: of the past, of the further past, and of all the pasts he had known.

Then the converter-cells cut off, the ship shuddered, and he knew they were inverspaced. The Minstrel sat up, his eyes far away. His thoughts were deep inside the cloud-cover of a world billions of light-years away, hundreds of years lost to him. A world he would never see again.

There was a time for running, and a time for resting, but even in the running there could be resting. He smiled to himself so faintly it was not a smile.

Down in the reactor rooms, they heard his song. They heard the build of it, matching, sustaining, ringing in harmony with the inverspace drive. They grinned at each other with a softness their faces did not seem equipped to wear.

'It's gonna be a good trip,' said one to another, smiling.

In the officer's country, Quantry looked up at the tight-slammed shields blocking off the patchwork insanity of not-space, and *he* smiled. It *was* going to be a good trip.

In the saloons, the passengers listened to the odd strains of lonely music coming up from below, and even they were forced to admit, though they had no way of explaining how they knew, that this was indeed going to be a good trip.

And in steerage, his fingers wandering across the keyboard of the battered theremin, no one noticed that the man they called the Minstrel had lit his cigarette without a match.

Blind Lightning

When Kettridge bent over to pick up the scurrying red lizard, the thing that had been waiting, struck.

Thought: *this is the prelude to the Time of Fast. In bulk this strangely-formed will equal many cat-litters. It is warm and does not lose the Essence. When the Essence-Stealer screams from the heavens, this strangely-formed will be many feastings for me. Safety and assured Essence are mine. O boon at last granted! To the Lord of the Heaven I turn all thought! Lad-nar's Essence is yours at Ending!*

The thing rose nine feet on powerfully-muscled legs; it had a sheened, glistening fur. It resembled a gorilla and a Brahma bull and a Kodiak bear and a number of other Terran animals, but it was none of them. The comparison was as inaccurate and brief as the moment Kettridge half-turned. He saw one of the thing's huge paws crashing toward him. The brief moment ended and Kettridge lay unconscious.

The huge beast bent from the waist and scooped up the man in the form-fitting metallic suit, brushing in annoyance at the belt of tools around the human's waist.

Lad-nar looked over one massive shoulder at the sky.

Even as he watched, the roiling dark clouds split and a forked brilliance stabbed down at the jungle. Lad-nar squinted his eyes, unconsciously lowering the thin secondary lids over them, filtering out the worst of the light.

He shivered as the roar screamed across the sky.

Off to his left another blast of lightning fingered down, struck a towering blue plant with a shower of sparks and a dazzling flash. Thunder bubbled after it. The jungle smoked.

Thought: *many risings and settings of the Great Warmer it has taken this Time of Fast to build. Now it will last for many more. The Great Warmer will be hidden and the cold will settle across the land. Lad-nar must find his way to the Place of Fasting. This strangely-formed will be many feastings.*

He shoved the man under one furry arm, clasping his unconscious burden tightly. Lad-nar's eyes were frightened. He knew the time of Death and Forbidden Walking was at hand.

He loped off toward the mountains.

The first thing Kettridge saw when he awoke was the head of the beast. It was hanging suspended in the light from the storm. The roar of the rain pelting down in driving sheets, the brilliant white light of the lightning, all served as background for the huge beast's head. That wide, blunt nose, three flaring nostrils. The massive double-lidded eyes—light from the fires outside blazing up in them like twin flickering comets. The high, hairy brow. The deep-black half-moons under the cheekbones.

The mouth of ripping, pointed teeth.

Kettridge was a man past the high tide of youth. He was not a strong man. At the beast's snort, the white-haired Earthman fainted.

It was a short stretch of unconsciousness. Kettridge blinked several times and tried to push himself up on elbows alarmingly weak. The sight that greeted him was substantially the same as before.

Lad-nar was still sitting, powerfully muscled legs

crossed, inside the mouth of the small cave, staring at him. Only the monstrous, frightening head, with pointed ears aprick, hanging there immobile.

'What—what—*are* you? We weren't expecting anything this large. The—the—survey said——' Kettridge quavered into silence.

Thought: *what is this? This strangely-formed speaks in my head! This is not one with the cat-litters. They cannot speak! Is this a symbol, an omen, from the Lord of the Heaven?*

What is it you ask, strangely-formed?

Kettridge felt the surge of thoughts in his mind. Felt it smash up against one nerve after another, sliding down and down in his head as the thoughts reverberated like an echo from far away. Over and over again.

'My God, the thing is telepathic!'

Old Kettridge knew it at once. He knew it because he had never experienced it before, and there was no doubting it. There had been a first time for everything for him. He knew the first time he had touched fire. He had known instantly it was fire, it would always be fire, and he must not touch it again.

He had known the first time love spoke to him. That had been once and never again. But he had known it the once it did speak.

There are those things which Man senses but once, and knows them—under whatever names he has assigned them—for what they are.

'You're telepathic!' he said again, hardly daring to believe it was true.

Thought: *what is that? What do you speak of, strangely-formed? What is that you say, that I hear as Reading Of the Essence? How is it you speak? Are you from the Lord of the Heaven?*

Lad-nar's thick, leathery lips had not moved. The fanged mouth had not twisted in speech. To Kettridge it seemed there was a third being in the cave. The hideous beast before him, himself . . . and a third. A speaker who roared in his mind, in a voice sharp and alert.

Thought: *there is no one else here. The is the Place of Fasting. Lad-nar has cleansed this place of all previous Fasting Ones. You do not answer. There is fear mixed into your Essence, like the cat-litters. Yet you are not one with them. Speak! Are you an omen?*

Kettridge's lips began to tremble. He looked intently at the great hulk across from him. The Earthman had suddenly realized that the being was not only telepathic, but two-way receptive. It could not only direct its thoughts into Kettridge's mind, it could just as easily pluck the ideas from the Earthman's head.

This was no animal.

This was no beast.

This was sentient life. If not of a high cultural level, at least of fantastic mental abilities.

'I—I am from Earth,' ventured Kettridge, sliding up against the warm stone wall of the cave.

Thought: *The Heaven Home! I know, I know! O thankings! The Lord of the Heaven has sent you to me as many feastings.*

In the space of a few short seconds, as Lad-nar spoke in thoughts, Kettridge received a complete picture of the being's life. He knew there was a race on Blestone—many more like Lad-nar. All in a barbaric hiding state. The preliminary survey had not indicated any life of this sort. Obviously Lad-nar's race was dying off.

Kettridge tried to blank out his thoughts. He had to wait.

Thought: *you can not hide the speaking in my head.*

Kettridge became frantic. He knew what the thing planned for him. He received a sharp, cold mental image of the being crouched over his body, ripping an arm loose from its socket. The picture was *too* clear. He became ill, and the being's thoughts in his head reverberated a dislike of the Earthman's powers of imagination.

Thought: *you have seen the feasting. Yet you are not like the cat-litters that squeal fear, fear, fear all the time that I feast on them. If you are not to eat, omen from the Heaven Lord—what are you?*

Kettridge felt his throat muscles tighten. His hands inside the heat-resistant gloves clenched. He felt his age settle around him as though it was a heavy mantle. 'I'm an alien ecologist,' he said, knowing it would do no good.

Thought: *this has no meaning for me.*

'I'm from Earth. I'm from one of those——' Then he stopped, drawing breath in quickly, pulling the resilient hood of the suit against his mouth with the effort. The being could not possibly know about 'one of *those* out there.' It could not see the stars. Only occasionally could it see the sun. Only when the clouds parted. The dense cloud blanket of Blestone hid space forever from the eyes of this monstrous being.

Thought: *Urth! The Heaven Home! I know! I know!*

There was a jubilation, a happiness in the thoughts. Something incongruous and terrifying when the old man put them into the head of that great thing illuminated by the storm.

Yet there was a humanness, a warmth, also.

Thought: *now I will sleep. Later I will feast.*

With the single-minded simplicity of the aborigine the great beast put from its mind this revelation of its religion, and obeyed the commands of its body. Tired from hunting, Lad-nar began to sleep.

The thoughts dimmed and faded out of Kettridge's mind like smoke wraiths as the huge animal slipped onto its side, effectively blocking the open mouth of the cave.

In a moment, they were gone entirely from Kettridge's suddenly throbbing head. The beast known as Lad-nar was asleep.

Kettridge felt for the service revolver at his belt. The charges in there were enough to stop a good-sized animal.

Then he looked at the nine feet of corded muscle and thick hide that lay there. He looked at the narrow confines of the cave. There was no chance to kill that beast before he could rip the Earthman to shreds.

...and did he really *want* to kill Lad-nar?

The thought bothered him. He knew he had to kill the beast—or be killed himself.

...and yet...

Outside the lightning boiled and crashed all around the cave. The long storm had begun.

Through the thin slit between the rocks and the beast, Kettridge could see the sky darkening and darkening as the storm grew. Every moment there was a new cataclysm of light and flash as streamers of fire flung themselves through the air. The night shattered itself against the rank jungle and howled in frenzy!

Kettridge rubbed his leathery, wrinkled cheek. The metal-plastic hood of the suit rubbed against the skin. 'I'd have been blistered and boiled,' he muttered, looking at the sleeping Lad-nar.

Blestone's atmosphere was an uncomfortable-to-humans 140–150° Fahrenheit. That would make the beast's body heat somewhere near 130 degrees. Which would have effectively ruined the aging career of Benjamin Kettridge, had not the Earthman's insulated suit protected him.

The old man hunched up small against the wall, feeling the rough stone through the suit. It somehow reassured him.

He knew the beam from the *Jeremy Bentham* was

tuned to the suit-sensitive, but they wouldn't come to pick him up till his search time was finished, and that was a good six hours away. He wasn't the only ecologist from the studyship on Blestone, but they were a low-pay outfit and they got the most for their money by leaving the searchers in solitude for the full time.

The full time had another six hours to run.

More than enough time for Lad-nar to get hungry.

He ran the whole thing through his mind, sifting the facts, gauging the information, calculating the outcome. It didn't look good.

He knew more about Lad-nar than the beast could have told him, though. That was a factor in his favor. He knew about its religion, its taboos, its—and here he felt his throat dry out again—eating habits, its level of intelligence and culture. The beast had thought it, had thought it all, and Kettridge had received it all.

Not quite what you signed up for, is it, Ben? he thought. Startled first at the muddiness of his own mental speech, he answered himself wearily, *No, not at all.*

Kettridge wondered what Lad-nar would think were he to tell the creature he wasn't the blue plate special, but a washed-out, run-down representative of a civilization that didn't give one hoot in Hell about Lad-nar or his religion. That didn't even care if his race died away.

He'd probably chew me up and swallow me, thought Kettridge. Then he added, *which is exactly what he'll do anyhow.*

It seemed so strange. Two day ago he had been aboard the *Jeremy Bentham*, study-ship one year out of Capitol City, and here he was today, main course at a Blestonian aborigine's feast.

The laughter wouldn't come.

It wouldn't come because Kettridge was old, and tired, and he knew how right it was that he die here, in this way. It was a fit end. It was somehow right in a Greater Scheme of Things. Lad-nar was doing all he knew. He was protecting himself. He was surviving.

Which is more than you've been doing for the last ten years, Ben, he told himself. Benjamin Kettridge had long ago stopped surviving. He knew it as clearly as he knew he would die here on this hot and steaming world far from the sight of Earth. *I'm glad I'm dying out of sight of that Sun.*

Think about it, Ben. Think it over. Now that it's all finished and you tumble out of things at fifty-six years of age. Think about it. Think about the waste, and the crying and the bit of conviction that could have saved you. Think about it all.

Then the story unfurled on a fleeting banner. It rolled out for Ben Kettridge there in a twilight universe. In a matter of a few minutes he had found life in that shadowy mind-world preferable to his outside existence.

He saw himself as a prominent scientist, engaged with others of his kind on a project of consequence to mankind. He saw his own worry and nagging anxiousness at the danger in the experiment.

He heard again the talk with Fenimore. He heard it more clearly than the blast and rush of the thunder outside.

'Charles, I don't think we should do it this way. If something were to happen...'

'Ben, you old bug, you! Nothing whatever can possibly happen—except what we want to happen. The Compound is as safe as breast milk, and you know it. There's no reason why everyone should know about it before we use it, though. That damned government has a way of pooh-poohing every major development, corrupting it, putting it off, worrying over it.

'First we demonstrate its applicability—*then* we let

the dunderheads scream about it. After they know its worth, they'll build monuments to us!'

'But don't you understand, Fenimore? There are too many random factors in the formulae. There's a fundamental flaw in there—if I could—only—figure it out.'

'Get this, Ben. I don't mean to pull seniority on you, but you force me. I'm not a harsh man, but this is a dream I've had for twenty years, and no piddling pen-scratching on your part is going to put it off. We test the Compound Thursday!'

It had been a dream for Fenimore. A dream that had overnight turned into a nightmare of twenty-five thousand dead, and hospitals stacked eight deep with screaming, intestine-twisted patients, howling for death rather than the suffering.

The nightmare had reached out clammy, thready tentacles and dragged in Kettridge, too. In a matter of days a reputation built of years of privation and sweat was reduced to rubble. Kettridge had barely escaped the mass lynchings. But he did not escape the inquests. What little reputation he had left had saved him—and a few others—from the gas chambers. But Life...

Life was at an end for him.

Ten years of struggling to eat, barely keeping alive—for no one would hire one of the men who had caused the Mass Death—had sunk Kettridge lower and lower. There was still a common decency about him that prevented a slump into some gutter, just as there was an inner desire to continue living. Even Life as it was to him then. Kettridge never became—as the others who escaped—a flophouse rummy or a suicide. He just became anonymous.

Lower and lower. Till there was nothing lower except slashed wrists or the bottle.

Kettridge had been too old, by then, for either.

And always there had been the knowledge that he could have stopped the project, had he voiced his doubts, instead of brooding in silence.

Finally the study-ship post had come. Ben Kettridge, with another name, had signed on. Three years, out to the stars, the cramp and squalor of shipboard, studying and cataloging. It hadn't been good, but it was a way to keep going.

Besides, how could he face the sun of Earth many more days—with *that* on his conscience?

So Ben Kettridge had become an alien ecologist. One year out from Capitol City, and *this*!

He wanted to scream. He wanted to scream very badly. His throat muscles drew up and tightened inside the wrinkled neck. His mouth, inside the flexible hood, opened wide, till the corners stretched in pain.

The pictures had stopped. He had withdrawn in terror from the shadowed mind-world, and he was back in a stone prison with a hungry aborigine for keeper.

His mind was a shrieking torrent of horror and futility and self-hatred. It was all a vortex, drawing his brain down into a black chasm. Oh, if he could only scream!

Lad-nar stirred.

The huge furred body twisted, snorted softly, and sank back into sleep. Kettridge wondered momentarily if the strength of his thoughts had disturbed the beast.

What a fantastic creature, thought Kettridge. *He lives on a world where the heat will fry a human and shivers in fear at lightning storms.*

A strange compassion came over Kettridge. How very much like a native of Earth this creature was. Governed by its stomach and a will to survive. A religion founded in fear and nurtured on terror. Lightning: the beast thought of it as a Screamer From the Skies. The occasionally glimpsed sun: The Great Warmer.

Kettridge pondered on the simplicity and common

sense of Lad-nar's religion.

When the storms gathered, finally building up enough charge to begin the lightning and thunder, Lad-nar knew the cold would set in. Cold was anathema to him. He knew the cold sapped him of strength, the lightning struck him down. So he stole a cat-litter and hid for the weeks it would take the gigantic storms to abate. The high body heat of the creature dictated that it have much food to keep it alive when the temperature went down. When a cat-litter wasn't handy, why then just *kill and eat an alien ecologist.* Kettridge found the last thought standing out in his mind.

This was no stupid beast, Kettridge reminded himself. His religion was a sound combination of animal wisdom and native observation. The lightning killed: don't go abroad in the storms. The storms brought cold: get food and stay alive.

It was so simple to analyze the situation. Simple, yes, but impossible to get himself out of it!

Not that I care, Kettridge mused.

I stopped caring long ago. The urge to survive? He laughed aloud. To his mind came the picture of himself. Thin, weary-looking. As though a world of agony had seeped like sand into his bones. His face was a lined and broken thing. It was tired. From the gray hair to the cleft chin. From the broken bridge of the aquiline nose to the thinned, parched lips. *I'm older than fifty-six*, he thought. There were men of fifty-six, he knew, who were still following the trails of the young.

I'm too sorry for myself.

It seemed strange. He had never churned these thoughts around in just this manner before. He had been prepared, almost eager, to let himself be beaten down, to be trampled under feet of sadness and self-pity. He was waiting for the creature to waken, then it would be at an end...

It was indeed strange how an odd situation could bring a man to a realization of himself.

Here is a chance, he thought. The words came unbidden.

In just these words. Here is a chance. Here was a chance not only to survive—something he had long since stopped doing consciously—but a chance to reinstate himself. If only in his own mind. Here was an aborigine, member of a dying race, a cowering beast of the caves, afraid to walk in the storms, in fear of the lightning, shackled by a primitive religion. Doomed forever to the land, never to see the sky.

In that split moment Ben Kettridge devised a plan to save his soul.

There are times when men sum up their lives. Take accounting and find themselves wanting. This was one of those times. So hopeless did it seem, that Ben Kettridge told himself, *This is a chance.*

Lad-nar suddenly became a symbol of all the people who had been lost in the Mass Death. In the mind of an old and tired man, many things are possible.

I must get out of here! Ben Kettridge told himself, over and over, almost as an incantation.

But more than that he knew he must save the poor hulk before him. And in saving the animal, he would save himself. Lad-nar had no idea what a star was. Well, Ben Kettridge would tell him. Here was a chance! Here was a chance!

The old man slid up flat against the wall. His back was strained with the effort to sink into the stone. Watching the alien beast come to wakefulness was almost the epitome of horror.

The huge body tossed and heaved, then rose. Directly. It sat erect from the thin, pinched waist, raising the massive wedge-shaped chest, the hideous head, the powerful neck and arms. A thin trickle of sleep-spittle dripped from a corner of its fanged mouth. It sat up and

Thought: *Lad-nar hungers.*

'Oh, God in Heaven, please let me have time! Please allow me this—this—*little* thing! I beg you!'

Kettridge found himself with hands clasped on his chest, face raised to the roof of the cave. For the first time in his life he felt tears of appeal on his cheeks.

He spoke to God with the tongue of a man who has never known a God. Science had been his deity—and that God had turned against him. He spoke from a heart so long full of misery and wandering it never knew it *could* speak to a God.

Thought: *You speak to the Lord of the Heaven.* Lad-nar seemed awed. It watched, its huge brilliant eyes suddenly unslitted and wide.

Kettridge thought at the beast.

Lad-nar! I come from the Lord of the Heaven. I am a God greater than the God in the Heaven! I can show you how to walk in the storms! I can show you how to——

The creature's roar deafened Kettridge. Along with it came the mental scream! The old man felt himself lifted off the floor by the force of that blow to the mind, and hurled against the rocks. His body burned and ached from the pounding, but he knew it had been his own reflexes that had done it.

The aborigine leaped to his feet, threw his taloned hands upward and bellowed his rage.

Thought: *you speak that which is Forbidden! You say that which is Untrue and Unclean! No human walks when the Essence-Stealer speaks in the night! You are a fearful thing! Lad-nar is afraid!*

'Heresy. I've spoken heresy!' Kettridge wanted to rip off the metal-plastic hood and tear his tongue from his own mouth. This was the way he had begun his own salvation! Heresy!

Thought: *yes, you have spoken that which is Unclean and Untrue!*

Kettridge cowered in fear. The beast was enraged. How could it be afraid, when it stood there so powerful and so massive?

Thought: *yes, Lad-nar is afraid! Afraid! Afraid!*

Then the waves of fear hit him. Kettridge felt his head begin to throb. The tender fiber of his mind was being twisted and seared and buffeted. Washed and burned and scarred forever with the terrible all-consuming fear the animal had coursing through itself.

Stop, stop, Lad-nar! I speak truth! I speak truth!

He spoke, then. Softly, winningly, trying to convince a being that had never known any God but one that howled and slashed in streamers of electricity. He spoke of himself. He spoke of his powers. He spoke of them as though he believed he had them. To himself he thought the things he was saying. He built himself a glory on two levels.

Slowly, Lad-nar calmed, and the waves of fear diminished to ripples. The awe and trembling remained, but there was a sliver of belief.

Kettridge knew he must work on that.

All too easily, down somewhere in his own mind, came back the picture of that huge creature, ripping and eating, ripping and eating...

'I come from the Heaven-Home, Lad-nar. I speak in the words of a God, for I am a God. A stronger God than the puny Essence-Stealer you fear!' As if to punctuate his words, a flash of lightning struck just outside the cave, filling the hollow with fury and light.

Kettridge continued, spilling the words faster and faster. 'I can walk abroad in the storm, and the Essence-Stealer will not harm me. Let me go out and I will show you, Lad-nar.' He was playing a dangerous hand; at any moment the beast might leap. It might dare to venture that leap hoping Kettridge was speaking falsely, rather than incur the wrath of a God he *knew* was dangerous.

Kettridge continued talking.

'Let me out, Lad-nar. Let me walk from this cave. I will show you.' He edged toward the cave's mouth, his hands in their metal-plastic gloves flat to the wall.

He knew the insulated suit would protect him from the viciousness outside.

Thought: *stop!*

'Why, Lad-nar? I can show you. I can show you how to walk in the night when the Essence-Stealer screams, and you can scream back at him and laugh at him, Lad-nar.' He didn't know why he was talking, he could have thought it just as well but there was a reassurance in the sound of his voice in the cave.

The old man felt the weariness seeping through his body. *Oh, if I was a younger man. If it wasn't so late!*

Thought: *Lad-nar does not know what less age means, but why should I let you go? You may have been sent by the Lord of the Heaven to see if I should lose my Essence. The Lord of the Heaven may be trying to take you back from me because I listened to your Unclean and Untrue sayings. Then I will have no feastings! Then I will lose my Essence!*

Kettridge reminded himself that the beast was indeed clever. Not only did it fear the wrath of the Lord of the Heaven and his screaming death, but Lad-nar knew if he let the man go he would have nothing to eat during the coming cold days.

'Let me go, Lad-nar. I will bring you back a cat-litter for your feasting. I will show you that I can walk in the night and I will bring you food. I will bring back a cat-litter, Lad-nar!' He prayed, silently, it would work.

Thought: *if you are a God, why do you speak to the Lord of the Heaven?*

Kettridge bit his lip. He kept forgetting . . .

He stopped thinking. He blocked it off. He willed himself to stop thinking. He must let his instincts answer for him.

'Because I want the Lord of the Heaven to know that I am as great as he and not afraid of him and that my prayers to him are only to show that I am as great as he.' It was gibberish, but it was a deep gibberish, and if he kept talking, the beast would shuck off the thoughts rather than try to fathom them.

The Earthman knew he had one factor in his favor: Lad-nar had never heard anyone speak against the Gods, and so one who did it and did not get blasted *must* be a God.

Kettridge hit him with the appeal again, before the animal had time to wonder.

'I'll get you a cat-litter, Lad-nar. Let me go! Let me show you! Let me show you that you can walk in the storms as I do! I, too, am a great God!' There was so much at stake here, so little time, so deep a Hell waiting.

Thought: *you will go away.*

There was a petulance, a little child sound, to the objection, and Kettridge knew the first step had been achieved.

'No, Lad-nar. Here is a rope.' He drew a thin cord of tough metal-plastic from his utility belt. His hand jiggled against the service revolver on his tool belt and he laughed deep inside once more as he thought of how useless it was.

Useless. Only in his wits was there salvation.

He would not have used the gun in any case. There was more at stake here than just his life.

'Here is a rope,' he repeated, extending the coiled cord. 'I will tie it about myself, like this . . . and . . . now! You take this end. Hold it tightly so that I can't escape. It is long enough so that I may go out and seek a cat-litter and show you I can walk abroad.'

At first the native refused, eyeing the glistening, silvery cord with fear in his deeply-pooled eyes. But Kettridge spoke on two levels, and spoke, and spoke, and soon the beast touched the cord.

It drew back its seven-taloned hand quickly.

The third time it grasped the cord.

You have just lost your religion, Kettridge thought.

Lad-nar had 'smelled' with his mind. He had sensed a cat-litter fairly close to the cave. But he did not know where.

Kettridge stepped out of the dark mouth of the cave, into the roaring maelstrom of a Blestonian electrical storm.

The sky was a tumult of heavy black clouds, steel and ebony and ripped dirty cloth. The clouds tumbled over themselves and died split apart as a bolt crashed through. The very air was charged, and blast after blast of lightning sheared away the atmosphere in zig-zagged streamers.

Kettridge stood with legs apart, body tilted forward against the pull of the cord, hands shading his eyes against the glare, the almost continuous glare, of lightning eruptions.

He was a small, thin man, and had it not been for the cord, he might easily have been swept away by the winds and rain that sandpapered the rocky ledge.

Streamers, branches, forks—the illumination of the arcing bolts was something magnificent and terrible. The old man stood there with the pelting rain washing over him, obscuring his vision through the hood, leaving only the glare of the storm for him.

He took a step, two, three.

The bolt slashed at him through a rift in the mountains. It roared over the precipice and streaked at him. It materialized out of nowhere and everywhere, splintering the stones at his feet. The rock flew up in planed, smoothed slivers, shooting in every direction. Kettridge fell flat and the crack of thunder rolled in on him. He realized it had come with the lightning, that he had been listening to it for almost a minute, before he realized what it was.

The effect on his body was sudden.

Immediately he went deaf. His skin began to prickle with the feel of a million tiny threads pushed into the flesh. His legs and hips were numb, his eyes reflected coruscating pinwheels of brilliance. He could see nothing but light on light inside light over light light light light...

There was a paralysis of his bladder.

Thought: *God! You are no God! The Essence-Stealer has screamed and you have fallen!*

The rope tightened and Kettridge felt himself being dragged back into the cave.

'No!' he screamed hurriedly. The pressure eased, 'No, Lad-nar. That was the Essence-Stealer's scream. Now I shall have mine. I *am* a God, I tell you! Let me show you, Lad-nar!'

Then he seized on the lightning blast for his own purpose. 'See, Lad-nar! The Essence-Stealer has struck me, but I am still whole. I will rise and walk again. You will see!'

Everywhere the lightning burned and crashed. The whole world was filled with the noise of frothing air and ripping jungle and screaming elements.

He clawed himself to his knees. His legs were weak and numb. The prickling was still there, but lessened. His eyes were starting to unglare and focus again. He still could hear nothing. He half-rose, sank back to one knee, rose again.

His head felt terribly heavy and unanchored.

Then he stood erect.

And he walked.

The storm raged about him. Lightning struck and struck again. Near him, to the side of him, behind him. One bolt sizzled down and struck him directly. The metal insulating suit served its purpose a second time. The bolt slashed, hit, and side-flashed off, exploding a small wizened tree growing up through a crack in the rocks. The tree flew into the air, one whole side charred and burned, the other unscarred.

It fell with a crash directly across Kettridge's path.

The symptoms of lightning-stroke were multiplied many times in Kettridge, but there was no answering thought of scorn from Lad-nar. Obviously the beast had withdrawn from his mind, in fear.

And he walked.

Soon he came back to the cave.

Thought: *you are a God! This I believe. But the Lord of the Heaven has sent his Essence-Stealers. They, too, are mighty, and Lad-nar will lose his Essence if he walks there.*

'No, Lad-nar. I will show you how to protect yourself.' The old man was sweating and white from his walk, and the numbness extended through his body. He could hear nothing, but the words came clearly to him.

He began to unseal the form-fitting suit.

The storm had already lowered the temperature enough so that he knew he would not fry.

In a few minutes he had the suit off, and it had shrunk back to a pocket-sized replica of the full-sized garment.

Kettridge felt ill. He felt old and tired and used. It was time to go home, time to quit. It was all over. He had won.

'Lad-nar, take this. Here, give me your hand.'

The beast looked at him with huge, uncomprehending eyes. The old man felt closer, somehow, to this strange creature than to anyone he had ever known. Kettridge pulled his glove on tighter and reached for Lad-nar's seven-taloned hand. He pulled at the arm of the form-fit suit, and it elastically expanded.

After much stretching and fitting, the beast was encased in the insulating metal-plastic.

Kettridge wanted to laugh at the bunched fur and awkward stance of the massive animal. But again, the laughter would not come.

'Now, Lad-nar, put on the gloves. Never take them off, except when the storms are gone. Always put this God-suit on when the Essence Stealers scream, and you will be safe.'

Thought: *now I can walk in the night?*

'Yes. Come.' He moved toward the cave's mouth. 'Now you can get a cat-litter for yourself. I did not bring one because I knew you would believe me and get your own. Come, Lad-nar.' He motioned the beast to follow him out into the rocks.

Thought: *how will you walk without the God-suit?*

Kettridge ran a seamed hand through his white hair. He was glad Lad-nar had thought the question. The multiple flashes of a many-stroked blast filled the air with glare and noise.

Kettridge could not hear the noise.

'I have God-brothers who wait for me in the Great House From Across the Skies that will take me back to the Heaven Home. They will hurry to me and they will protect me.'

He did not bother to tell the great beast that his search time was almost up and that the *Jeremy Bentham*'s flitter would home in on his suit beam. It would have been useless homing, had he not secured time.

'Go! Walk, Lad-nar!' he said, throwing his arms out as he felt a God would. 'And tell your bothers you have screamed at the Essence-Stealers!'

Thought: *I have done this.*

The great animal stepped cautiously toward the rocky ledge, fearful and hesitant. Then it bunched its huge muscles and leaped out into the full agony of the storm which crashed in futility about his massive form.

'One day Man will come and make friends with you, Lad-nar,' said the old man, softly. 'One day, they will come down out of the sky and show you how to live on this world of yours so that you don't have to hide.'

Kettridge sank down against the inner wall of the cave, suddenly too exhausted to stand.

He had won. He had redeemed himself. If only in his own mind. He had helped take some life from a race, yet he had given life to another race.

He closed his eyes peacefully. Even the great blasts of blind lightning did not bother him as he rested. He knew Lad-nar had told his brothers.

He knew the ship was coming for him.

Lad-nar came up the incline and saw the flitter streaking down, lightning playing along its sides in phosphorescent glimmers.

Thought: *God! God! Your God-brothers come for you!*

He bounded across the scarred and seared rocks, toward the cave.

Kettridge rose and stepped out into the rain and wind.

He ran a few steps, waving his arms in signal. The flitter altered course and headed for the old man.

The lightning struck.

It seemed as though the bolt knew its target. It raced the flitter, sizzling and burning as it came. In a roar of light and dark and screamings it tore at the old man, lifting him high into the air, charring and burning and ripping.

The body landed just outside the cave, blistered and bleeding. The old man was still alive...

Thought: *God! God! You have fallen! Rise, rise, rise! The Essence-Stealers...*

The thoughts were hysterical, tearful, torn and wanting. Had the beast been able to shed tears, Kettridge knew it would have done so. The old man lay sightless, eyes gone, senses altogether torn from him. The Essence ebbed.

He thought:

Lad-nar. There will come other Gods. They will come to you and you must think to them. You must think these words, Lad-nar. Think to them, show me a star. *Do you hear me, Lad-nar? Do you...*

Even as the great beast watched, the Essence flickered and died. In the animal's mind there was a lack, a space of emptiness. Yet there was a contentment. A peace, and Lad-nar knew the Essence of the God Who Walked In The Light was soft and unafraid at Ending.

The aborigine stood on the rocks below the cave and watched the flitter sink to the stone ledge. He watched as the other Gods From the Skies emerged and ran to the charred hulk lying on the stones.

Through his head, like the blind lightning, streaking everywhere, lightning, lightning, lightning, the words remained, and repeated...

Thought:

Show me a star.

All the Sounds of Fear

'Give me some light!'

Cry: tormented, half-moan half-chant, cast out against a whispering darkness: a man wound in white, arms upflung to roistering shadows, sooty sockets where eyes had been, pleading, demanding, anger and hopelessness, anguish from the soul into the world. He stumbled, a step, two, faltering, weak, the man returned to the child, trying to find some exit from the washing sea of darkness in which he trembled.

'Give me some light!'

Around him a Greek chorus of sussurating voices. Plucking at his garments he staggered toward an intimation of sound, a resting place, a goal. The man in pain, the figure of *all* pain, all desperation, and nowhere in that circle of painful light was there release from his torment. Sandaled feet stepping, each one above an abyss, no hope and no safety; what can it mean to be so eternally blind?

Again, 'Give me some light!'

The last tortured ripping of the words from a throat raw with the hopelessness of salvation. Then the man sank to the shadows that moved in on him. The face half-hidden in chiaroscuro, sharp black, blanched white, down and down into the grayness about his feet, the circle of blazing-white light pinpointing him, a creature impaled on a shard of brilliance, till closing, closing,

closing it swallowed him, all gone to black, darkness within and without, black even deeper, nothing, finis, end; silence.

Richard Becker, Oedipus, had played his first role. Twenty-four years later, he would play it again, as his last. But before that final performance's curtain could be rung, twenty-four years of greatness would have to strut across stages of life and theater and emotion.

Time, passing.

When they had decided to cast the paranoid beggar in *Sweet Miracles*, Richard Becker had gone to the Salvation Army retail store and bought a set of rags that even the sanctimonious charity workers staffing the shop tried to throw out as unsaleable and foul. He bought a pair of cracked and soleless shoes that were a size too large. He bought a hat that had seen so many autumns of rain its brim had bowed and withered under the onslaught. He bought a no-color vest from a suit long since destroyed and a pair of pants whose seat sagged raggedly and a shirt with three buttons gone and a jacket that seemed to typify every derelict who had ever cadged an hour's sleep in an alley.

He bought these things over the protests of the kindly, white-haired women who were *doing their bit for charity*, and he asked if he might step into the toilet for a few moments to try them on; and when he emerged, his good tweed jacket and dark slacks over his arm, he was another man entirely. As though magically, coarse stubble had sprouted on his sagging jowls. (It may well have been there when he came into the shop, but who would have noticed? He was too nice-looking a young man to go around unshaved.) The hair had grown limp and off-gray under the squashed hat. The face was lined and planed with the depravities and deprivations of a lifetime lived in gutters and saloons. The hands were caked with filth, the eyes lusterless and devoid of personality, the body grotesquely slumped by the burden of mere existence. This old man, this skid from the Bowery, how had he gotten into the toilet, and where was the nice young man who had gone in wearing that jacket and those slacks? Had this *creature* somehow overpowered him (what foul weapon had this feeble old man used to subdue a vital, strong youth like that)? The white-haired Good Women of Charity were frozen with distress as they imagined the strong-faced, attractive youth, lying in the bathroom, his skull crushed by a length of pipe.

The old bum extended the jacket, the pants, and the rest of the clothing the young man had been wearing, and in a voice that was thirty years younger than the body from which it spoke, he explained, 'I won't be needing these, ladies. Sell them to someone who can make good use of them.' The voice of the young man, from this husk.

And he paid for the rags he wore. They watched him as he limped and rolled through the front door into the filthy streets, another tramp gone to join the tide of lost souls that would inevitably become a stream and a river and an ocean of wastrels, washing finally into a drunk tank or a doorway or a park bench.

Richard Becker spent six weeks living on the Bowery; in fleabags, abandoned warehouses, cellars, gutters, and on tenement rooftops; he shared and wallowed in the nature and filth and degradation of the empty men of his times.

For six weeks he *was* a tramp, a thoroughly washed-out hopeless rumdum, with rheumy eyes and palsied hands and a weak bladder.

One by one the weeks mounted to six, and on the first day of casting for *Sweet Miracles*, the Monday of the seventh week, Richard Becker arrived at the Martin Theatre, where he auditioned for the part in the clothes he had worn for the past six weeks.

The play ran for five hundred and eighteen performances, and Richard Becker won the Drama Critics' Circle Award as the finest male performer of the year. He also won the Circle Award as the most promising newcomer of the year.

He was twenty-two years old at the time.

The following season, after *Sweet Miracles* had gone on the road, Richard Becker was apprised, through the pages of *Variety*, that John Foresman & T. H. Searle were about to begin casting for *House of Infidels*, the posthumous script by Odets, the last he ever wrote. Through friends in the Foresman & Searle offices, he obtained a copy of the script, and selected a part he considered massive in its potentialities.

The role of an introspective and tormented artist, depressed by the level of commercialism to which his work had sunk, resolved to regain an innocence of childhood or nature he had lost, by working with his hands in a foundry.

When the first-night critics called Richard Becker's conception of Tresk, the artist, 'a pinnacle of thespic intuition' and noted, 'His authority in the part led members of the audience to ask one another how such a sensitive actor could grasp the rough unsubtle life of a foundry worker,' they had no idea that Richard Becker had worked for nearly two months in a steel stamping plant and foundry in Pittsburgh. But the makeup man on *House of Infidels* suspected Richard Becker had once been in a terrible fire, for his hands were marked by the ravages of great heat.

After two successes, two conquests of Broadway, two characterizations that were immediately ranked with the most brilliant Shubert Alley had ever witnessed, Richard Becker's reputation began to build a legend.

The Man Who IS The 'Method,' they called him, in

perceptive articles and interviews. Lee Strasberg of the Actors' Studio, when questioned, remarked that Becker had never been a student, but had the occasion arisen, he might well have paid *him* to attend. In any event, Richard Becker's command of the Stanislavski theory of total immersion in a part became a working example of the validity of the concept. No mere scratcher and stammerer, Richard Becker *was* the man he pretended to be, on a stage.

Of his private life little was known, for he let it be known that if he was to be totally convincing in a characterization, he wanted no intrusive shadow of himself to stand between the audience and the image he offered.

Hollywood's offers of stardom were refused, for as *Theatre Arts* commented in a brief feature on Richard Becker:

'The gestalt that Becker projects across a row of footlights would be dimmed and turned two-dimensional on the Hollywood screen. Becker's art is an ultimate distillation of truth and metamorphosis that requires the reality of stage production to retain its purity. It might even be noted that Richard Becker acts in *four* dimensions, as opposed to the merely craftsmanlike three of his contemporaries. Surely no one could truly argue with the fact that watching a Becker performance is almost a religious experience. We can only congratulate Richard Becker on his perceptiveness in turning down studio bids.'

The years of building a backlog of definitive parts (effectively ruining them for other actors who were condemned to play them after Becker had said all there was to say) passed, as Richard Becker became, in turn, a Hamlet that cast new lights on the Freudian implications of Shakespeare ... a fiery Southern segregationist whose wife reveals her octaroon background ... a fast-talking salesman come to grips with futility and cowardice . . . a many-faceted Marco Polo . . . a dissolute and totally amoral pimp, driven by a loathing for women, to sell his own sister into evil . . . a ruthless politician, dying of cancer and senility . . .

And the most challenging part he had ever undertaken, the recreation, in the play by Tennessee Williams, of the deranged religious zealot, trapped by his own warring emotions, into the hammer-murder of an innocent girl.

When they found him, in the model's apartment off Gramercy Place, they were unable to get a coherent story of why he had done the disgusting act, for he had lapsed into a stentorian tone of Biblical fervor, pontificating about the blood of the lamb and the curse of Jezebel and the eternal fires of Perdition. The men from Homicide numbered among their ranks a rookie, fresh to the squad, who became desperately ill at the sight of the fouled walls and the crumpled form wedged into the tiny kitchenette; he became violently ill, and was taken from the apartment a few minutes before Richard Becker was led away.

The trial was a manifest sadness to all who had seen him onstage, and the jury did not even have to be sent out to agree on a verdict of insanity.

After all, whoever the fanatic was that the defense put on the stands, he was not sane, and was certainly no longer Richard Becker, the actor.

For Dr. Charles Tedrow, the patient in restraining room 16 was a constant involvement. He was unable to divorce himself from the memory of a night three years before, when he had sat in an orchestra seat at the Henry Miller Theatre and seen Richard Becker, light and adroit, as the comical Tosspot in that season's hit comedy, *Never A Rascal.*

He was unable to separate his thoughts from the shape and form of the actor who had so immersed himself in The Method that for a time, in three acts, he *was* a blundering, maundering, larcenous alcholic with a penchant for pomegranates and (as Becker had mouthed it onstage) 'barratry on the low seas!' Separate them from this weird and many-faceted creature that lived its many lives in the padded cell numbered 16? Impossible.

At first, there had been reporters, who had come to interview the Good Doctor in charge of Becker's case; and to the last of these (for Dr. Tedrow had instituted restrictions on this sort of publicity) he had said, 'To a man like Richard Becker, the world was very important. He was very much a man of his times; he had no real personality of his own, with the exception of that one overwhelming faculty and need to reflect the world around him. He was an actor in the purest sense of the word. The world gave him his personality, his attitudes, his reason and his facade for existence. Take those away from him, clap him up in a padded cell—as we've been forced to do—and he begins to lose touch with reality.'

'I understand,' the reporter had inquired carefully, 'that Becker is reliving his roles, one after another. Is that true, Dr. Tedrow?'

Charles Tedrow was, above all else, a compassionate man, and his fury at this remark, revealing as it did a leak in the sanitarium's security policy, was manifest. 'Richard Becker is undergoing what might be called, in psychiatric terms, "induced hallucinatory regression." In his search for some reality, there in that room, he has fastened onto the method of assuming characters' moods he had played onstage. From what I've been able to piece together from reviews of his shows, he is going back from the most recent to the next and the next and so on.'

The reporter had asked more questions, more superficial and phantasmagoric assumptions, until Dr. Charles Tedrow had concluded the interview rudely.

But even now, as he sat across from Richard Becker in the quiet office, he knew that almost nothing the reporter had conceived, could rival what Becker had done to himself.

'Tell me, Doctor,' the florid, bombastic traveling salesman who was Richard Becker asked, 'what the hell's new down the line?'

'It's really very quiet, these days, Ted,' the physician replied. Becker had been this way for two months now: submerged in the part of Ted Rogat, the loudmouth philandering protagonist of Chayefsky's *The Wanderer*. For six months before that he had been Marco Polo, and before that the nervous, slack-jawed and incestuous son of *The Glass of Sadness*.

'Hell, I remember one little chippie in, where was it, oh yeah, hell yes! It was K.C. good old K.C. man, she was a *goodie*! You ever been to K.C., Doc? I was a drummer in nylons when I worked K.C. Jeezus, lemme tell ya——'

It was difficult to believe the man who sat on the other side of the table was an actor. He looked the part, he spoke the part, he *was* Ted Rogat, and Dr. Tedrow could catch himself from time to time contemplating the release of this total stranger who had wandered into Richard Becker's cell.

He sat and listened to the story of the flame-hipped harlot in Kansas City that Ted Rogat had picked up in an Armenian restaurant and seduced with promises of nylons. He listened to it, and knew that whatever else was true of Richard Becker, this creature of many faces and many lives, he was no saner than the day he had killed that girl. After eighteen months in the sanitarium, he was going back, back, back through his acting career, and replaying the roles, but never once coming to grips with reality.

In the plight and disease of Richard Becker, Dr. Charles Tedrow saw a bit of himself, of all men of his times, and the thousand illnesses to which they were heir.

He returned Richard Becker, as well as Ted Rogat, to the security and tiny world of Room 16.

Two months later he brought him back, and spent a highly interesting three hours discussing group therapy with Herr Doktor Ernst Loebisch, credentials from the Munich Academy of Medicine and the Vienna Psychiatric Clinic. Four months after that, Dr. Tedrow got to know the surly and insipid Jackie Bishoff, juvenile delinquent and hero of *Streets of Night.*

And almost a year later, to the day, Dr. Tedrow sat in his office with a bum, a derelict, a rheumy-eyed and dissipated vagabond who could only be the skid from *Sweet Miracles*, Richard Becker's first triumph, twenty-four years before.

What Richard Becker might look like, without camouflage, in his own shell, Tedrow had no idea. He was, now, to all intents and purposes, the seedy old tramp with the dirt caked into the sagged folds of his face.

'Mr. Becker, I want to talk to you.'

Hopelessness shined out of the old bum's eyes. There was no answer.

'Listen to me, Becker. Please listen to me, if you're in there somewhere, if you can hear me. I want you to understand what I'm about to say; it's very important.'

A croak, cracked and forced, came from the bum's lips, and he mumbled, 'I need'a drink, yuh go' uh drink fuh me, huh . . .'

Tedrow leaned across, his hand shaking as he took the old bum's chin in his palm, and held it fixed, staring into the stranger's eyes. 'Now listen to me, Becker. You've got to hear me. I've gone through the files, and as far as I can tell, this was the first part you ever played. I don't know what will happen! I don't know what form this syndrome will take after you've used up all your other lives. But if you can hear me, you've got to understand that you may be approaching a critical period in your—in your life.'

The old bum licked cracked lips.

'*Listen!* I'm here, I want to help you, I want to *do* something for you, Becker. If you'll come out for an instant, just a second, we can establish contact. It's got to be now or——'

He left it hanging. He had no way of knowing *if-what*. And as he lapsed into silence, as he released the bum's chin, a strange alteration of facial muscles began, and the derelict's countenance shifted, subtly ran like hot lead, and for a second he saw a face he recognized. From the eyes that were no longer red-rimmed and bloodshot, Dr. Charles Tedrow saw intelligence peering out.

'It sounds like fear, Doctor,' he said.

And, 'Goodbye, once more.'

Then the light died, the face shifted finally, and the physician was again staring at the empty face of a gutter-bred derelict.

He sent the old man back to Room 16. Later that day, he had one of the male nurses take in an 89c. bottle of muscatel.

Fear crackled across the telephone wires.

'Speak up, man! What in the name of God is going on out there?'

'I—I can't explain it, Dr. Tedrow, but you better—you better get out here right away. It's—it's oh Jee-zus!'

'What *is* it? Stop crying, Wilson, and tell me what the hell is *wrong*!'

'It's, it's number sixteen . . . it's . . .'

'I'll be there in twenty minutes. Keep everyone away

from that room. Do you understand? Wilson! Do you understand me?'

'Yessir, yessir. I'll—oh Christ—hurry up Doc . . .'

He could feel his pajama pants bunched around his knees, under his slacks, as he floored the pedal of the ranch wagon. The midnight roads were jerky in the windshield, and the murk through which he raced was almost too ominous to be a fact of nature.

When he slewed the car into the drive, the gatekeeper threw the iron barrier back almost spastically. The ranch wagon chewed gravel, sending debris back in a wide fan, as Tedrow plunged ahead. When he screeched to a halt in front of the sanitarium, the doors burst open and the Senior Attendant, Wilson, raced down the steps.

'This way, th-this way, Doctor Te——'

'Get out of my way, you idiot. I know which direction!' He shoved Wilson aside, and strode up the steps and into the building.

'It started about an hour ago . . . we didn't know what was happ——'

'And you didn't call me immediately? Ass!'

'We just thought, we just thought it was another one of his stages, *you* know how he is . . .'

Tedrow snorted in disgust and threw off his topcoat as he made his way rapidly down the corridor to the section of the sanitarium that housed the restraining rooms.

As they came into the annex, through the heavy glass-portaled door, he heard the scream for the first time.

In that scream, in that tormented, pleading, demanding and hopelessly lost tremor there were all the sounds of fear he had ever heard. In that voice he heard even his own voice, his own soul, crying out for something.

For an unnameable something, as the scream came again.

'Give me some light!'

Another world, another voice, another life. Some evil

and empty beseeching from a corner of a dust-strewn universe. Hanging there timelessly, vibrant in colorless agony. A million tired and blind stolen voices all wrapped into that one howl, all the eternal sadnesses and losses and pains ever known to man. It was all there, as the good in the world was sliced open and left to bleed its golden fluid away in the dirt. It was a lone animal being eaten by a bird of prey. It was a hundred children crushed beneath iron treads. It was one good man with his entrails in his blood-soaked hands. It was the soul and the pain and the very vital fiber of life, draining away, without light, without hope, without succor.

'Give me some light!'

Tedrow flung himself at the door, and threw back the bolt on the observation window. He stared for a long and silent moment as the scream trembled once more on the air, weightlessly, transparently, tingling off into emptiness. He stared, and felt the inpact of a massive horror stifle his own cry of disbelief and terror.

Then he spun away from the window and hung there, sweat-drenched back flat to the wall, with the last sight of Richard Becker he would ever hope to see, burned forever behind his eyes.

The sound of his soft sobs in the corridor held the others back. They stared silently, still hearing that never-spoken echo reverberating down and down and down the corridors of their minds:

Give me some light!

Fumbling beside him, Tedrow slammed the observation window shut, and then his arm sank back to his side.

While inside Room 16, lying up against the far wall, his back against the soft passive padding, Richard Becker looked out at the door, at the corridor, at the world, forever.

Looked out as he had come, purely and simply.

Without a face. From his hairline to his chin, a blank, empty, featureless expanse. Empty. Silent. Devoid of sight or smell or sound. Blank and faceless, a creature God had never deigned to bless with a mirror to the world. His Method now was gone.

Richard Becker, actor, had played his last part, and had gone away, taking with him Richard Becker, a man who had known all the sounds, all the sights, all the life of fear.

The Silver Corridor

'We can't be responsible for death or disfigurement, you know,' reminded the Duelmaster.

He toyed with the Company emblem on his ceremonial robe absently, waiting Marmorth's answer. Behind him, across the onyx and crystal expanse of the preparation chamber, the gaping maw of the Silver Corridor opened into blackness.

'Yes, yes, I know all that,' snapped Marmorth impatiently. 'Has Krane entered his end?' he asked, casting a glance at the dilation-segment leading to the adjoining preparation room. There was fear and apprehension in the look, only thinly hidden.

'Not quite yet,' the Duelmaster told him. 'By now he has signed the release, and they are briefing him, as I'm about to brief you, if you'll kindly sign yours.' He indicated the printed form in the trough, and the stylus on the desk.

Marmorth licked his lips, mumbled something half-heard, and flourished his signature on the blank line. The signing was done hurriedly, as though he was afraid he might forget his name, should he hesitate.

The Duelmaster glanced quickly at the signature, then pressed the stud on the desk top. The blank slipped out of sight in the trough. He carefully took the stylus from Marmorth's unfeeling fingers, placed it in his pouch. They waited patiently for a minute. A soft clucking came up through a slot in the side of the desk, and a second later a punched plastic plate dropped into a basket beneath it.

'This is your variation-range card,' explained the Duelmaster, lifting the plate from the basket. 'With this we can gauge the extent of your imagination, set up the illusions, send you through the Corridor at your own mental pace.'

'I understand perfectly, Duelsman,' snapped Marmorth. 'Do you mind getting me in there! I'm freezing in this breechclout!'

'Mr. Marmorth, I realize this is annoying, but we are required both by statute of law and rule of the Company to explain thoroughly the entire sequence, before entrance.' He stood up behind the desk, reached into a cabinet that dilated at the approach of his hand.

'Here,' he said, handing Marmorth a wraparound, 'put this on till we've finished here.'

Marmorth let breath whistle between his teeth in irritation, but donned the robe and sat back down in front of the desk. Marmorth was a man of medium height, hair graying slightly at the temples and forelock, a middle-aged stomach bulge. He had dark, not-quite-piercing eyes, and straight plain features. An undistinguished man, yet one who seemed to have a touch of authority and determination about him. An undistinguished man, a middle-aged man, a man about to enter a duel.

'As you know——' began the Duelmaster.

'Yes, yes, confound it! *I know, I know!* Why must you people prolong the agony of this thing?' Marmorth cut him off, rising again.

'Mr. Marmorth,' resumed the Duelmaster patiently but doggedly, 'if you don't settle yourself, we will call this Affair off. Do you understand?'

Marmorth chuckled ruefully, deep in his throat. 'After the tolls Krane and I laid out? You won't cancel.'

'We will if you aren't prepared for combat. It's for your own survival, Mr. Marmorth. Now if you'll be silent a minute, I'll brief you and you can enter the Corridor.'

Marmorth waved his hand negligently, grudging the Duelsman his explanation. He stared in boredom at the high crystal ceiling of the preparation chamber.

'The Corridor, *as you know,*' went on the Duelsman, adding the last phrase with sarcasm, 'is a supersensitive receptor. When you enter it, seven billion scanning elements pick up your thoughts, down to the very subconscious, filter them through the banks, correlating them with your variation-range card, and feed back illusions. These illusions are matched with those of your opponent, as checked with *his* variation-range card. The illusion is always the same for both of you.

'Since you are in the field of the Corridor, these are substantial illusions, and they affect you as though they were real. In other words, to illustrate the extreme—you can die at any moment. They are not dreams, I assure you. All too often combatants find an illusion so strange they feel it must be unreal. May I caution you, Mr. Marmorth, that is the quickest way to lose an Affair. Take everything you see at face value. *It is real!*'

He paused for a moment, wiping his forehead. He had begun to perspire freely. Marmorth wondered at this, but remained silent.

'Your handicap,' the Duelmaster resumed, 'is that when an illusion is formed from a larger segment of your opponent's imagination than from yours, he will be more familiar with it, and will be more able to get to you. The same holds true for him, of course.

'The illusions will strengthen for the combatant who is dominating. In other words, if Krane's outlook is firmer than yours, he will have a more familiar illusion. If you begin to dominate him, the illusion will change to one more of your making.

'Do you understand?'

Marmorth had found himself listening more intently than he thought he would. Now he had questions.

'Aren't there any weapons we begin with? I'd always thought we could choose our dueling weapons.'

The Duelmaster shook his head. 'No. There will be sufficient weapons in your illusions. Anything else would be superfluous.'

'How can an illusion kill me?'

'You are in the Corridor's field. Through a process of—well, actually, Mr. Marmorth, that is a Company secret, and I doubt if it could be explained in lay terms so that you would know any more now than you did before. Just accept that the Corridor converts your thought-impressions into tangibles.'

'How long will we be in there?'

'Time is subjective in the Corridor. You may be there for an hour or a month or a year. Out here the time will seem as an instant. You will go in, both of you, then a moment later—one of you will come out.'

Marmorth licked his lips again. 'Have there been duels where a stalemate was reached; where both combatants came back?' He was nervous, and the question trembled as if it was made with metallic filaments.

'We've never had one that I can recall,' answered the Duelmaster simply.

'Oh,' said Marmorth quietly, looking down at his hands.

'Are you ready now?'

Marmoth nodded. He slipped out of the wraparound and laid it across the back of the chair. Together they walked toward the Silver Corridor. 'Remember,' said the Duelmaster, 'the combatant who has the strongest convictions will win. This is a constant, and your only real weapon.'

The Duelmaster stepped to the end of the Corridor, removing a thin tube from his pouch. A beam of light flashed thinly from the end, and he shone it at an aperture in the wall next to the Corridor's opening.

The light flashed twice, then he said. 'I've signaled the Duelsman on the other side. Krane has been placed inside.'

The Duelmaster slipped the variation-range card into a slot in the blank wall, then indicated Marmorth should step into the Corridor.

The middle-aged duelist stepped forward, smoothing the short breechclout against his thighs as he walked.

He took one step, two, three. The perfectly round mouth of the Silver Corridor gaped before him, black and impenetrable.

He stepped forward once more. His bare foot touched the edge of the metal, and he drew back hesitantly. He looked back over his shoulder at the Duelsman. 'Couldn't I——'

'Step in, Mr. Marmorth,' said the Duelmaster firmly. There was a granite tone in his voice.

Marmorth walked forward into the darkness. It closed over his head and seeped behind his eyes. He felt nothing! Marmorth...

...blinked twice. The first time he saw the throne room and the tier-mounted pages, long-stemmed trumpets at their sides. He saw the assembled nobles bowing low before him, their ermine capes sweeping the floor. The floor was a rich, inlaid mosaic, the walls dripped color and rich tapestry, the ceiling was high-arched and studded with crystal chandeliers.

The second time he opened them, hoping his senses had cleared, he saw precisely the same thing. Then he saw Krane—High Lord Krane—in the front ranks.

The man's hair had been swept back to form a tight

knot at the base of his skull. It was the knot of the triumphant warrior. The garb was different—tight suit of chainmail in blued-steel, ornamental decorations across the breastplate, a ruby-hilted sword in a scabbard at his waist, full, flowing cape of blood-red velvet—but the face was no different from the one Marmorth had seen in the Council Chamber, before they had agreed to duel.

The face was thin; a V that swept past a high, white forehead and thick, black brows, past the high cheekbones and needle-thin nose, down to the slash mouth and pointed black beard. A study in coal and chalk.

Marmorth's blood churned at sight of the despised Krane! If he hadn't challenged Marmorth's Theorem in the Council Chamber, with his duel-inciting slanders, neither of them would be here.

Here!

Marmorth stiffened. He sat more erect. The knowledge swept away his momentary forgetfulness; this was the Silver Corridor. This was illusion. They *were* dueling—now, at this instant! He had to kill Krane.

But whose illusion was this? His own, or the dark-bearded scoundrel's before him? It might be suicide to attempt killing Krane in his own illusion. He would have to wait a bit and gauge what the situation represented in his own mind.

Whatever it was, he seemed to be of higher rank than Krane, who bowed before him.

Almost magically, before he realized the words were emerging from his mouth, he heard himself saying, 'Lord Krane, rise!'

Krane stood up, and the other nobles followed suit, the precedent having been set. By choosing Krane to rise first, Marmorth the King had chosen whom he wanted to speak first in the Star Chamber.

'May it please your Illustriousness,' boomed Krane, extending his arms in salute, 'I have a disposition on the prisoners from Quorth. I should beg your Eminence's verdict on my proposal.'

He bowed his head and waited Marmorth's reply.

Had there been a tone of mockery in the man's voice? Marmorth could not be sure. But he now knew that it was his own illusion. If Krane was coming to *him* for disposition, then he must be in the ascendant in this creation.

'What is your proposal, High Lord Krane?' asked Marmorth.

Krane took a step forward, bringing him to the bottom of the dais upon which Marmorth's throne rested.

'These *things* are of a totally alien culture, Your Highness,' began Krane. 'How can we, as humans, even tolerate their existence in our way of life? The very sight of them makes the gorge rise! They are evil-smelling and accursedly-formed! They must all be destroyed, Your Highness! We must ignore the guileful offers of a prisoner-for-prisoner exchange! We will have our fleet in Quorth City within months, then we can rescue our own captured without submitting to the demands of foul monsters! In the meantime, why feed these beasts of another world?

'I say, destroy them! Launch all-out attack now! Rescue our people from the alien's slave camps on Quorth and Fetsa!'

He had been speaking smoothly and forcefully. The nods of assent and agreement from the assembled nobles made Marmorth wary. A complete knowledge of the Quorth-Human war was in his mind, and the plan of Krane sounded clear and fine. Yet superimposed over it was his knowledge that this was all merely illusion and that somewhere in the illusion was a chink in which his errors might lodge. The plan sounded good, but . . .

'No, Krane!' he decided, thinking quietly. 'This would be what the aliens want! They *want* us to destroy our prisoners. That would whip their people at home into such a frenzy of patriotism—we would be engulfed in a month!

'We will consider the alien proposal of prisoner-for-prisoner exchange.' The rumbles from the massed nobles rose into the cavern of the Star Chamber. There was unrest here.

He had to demonstrate that he was right. 'Let them bring in the chain of aliens!' he commanded, clapping his hands. A page went out to summon them.

While the hall waited, Marmorth thought quickly: had he made the proper decision? There seemed to be a correlation between Krane's challenging of his Theorem of Government in the Council—back in the world outside the Corridor—and this proposal he had just defeated.

There *was* a correlation! He saw it suddenly!

Both his proposal of the Theorem in the Council and his decision here in the illusion had been based on his personal concept of government. Krane's refutation out there and his proposal here were the opposite. Once again they had clashed.

And this time Marmorth had won!

But had he?

Even as he let the thought filter, the chained aliens were dragged between the massed nobles and cast on their triple-jointed knees before Marmorth's dais. 'Here are the loathsome beings!' cried Krane, flinging his arms high and apart.

It had been a grandstand gesture, and the frog-faced, many-footed beings on the Star Chamber's floor realized it.

Suddenly, almost as though they were made of paper, the chains that had joined the aliens snapped, and they leaped on the nobles.

Marmorth caught the smile on Krane's lips. *He* had

been behind this; probably had the chains weakened in the corridor outside by his loyal personal guard.

Hardly with thought, Marmorth was off his throne and down the stepped dais, his sword free from its scabbard, and arching viciously.

A hideously warted alien face rose before him and he thrust with all his might! The blade pierced between the double-lidded eyes, and thick ochre blood spurted across his tunic. He yanked the blade free, kicking the dead but still quivering alien from its length. He leaped into the horde, howling a battlecry from his youth.

Even as he leaped, he saw Krane's slash-mouthed smile, and the Lord's sword swinging toward him!

So it *hadn't* been his illusion! It had been Krane's! He hadn't chosen the proper course. Krane's belief at the moment was stronger than his own.

He fended off a double-handed smash from the black-bearded noble and fell back. They parried and countered, thrust and slashed all around the dais. The other nobles were too deeply involved fighting off the screaming aliens to witness this battle between their King and his Lord.

Krane beat Marmorth back, back!

Why did I choose as I did? Marmorth wailed mentally, berating himself.

Suddenly he slipped, toppling backward onto the steps. The sword flew from his hand as it cracked against the edge of a step. He saw Krane bearing down on him, the sword double-fisted as his opponent raised it like a stake above his head.

In desperation, Marmorth summed up all his belief. '*It was the right decision!*' screamed Marmorth with the conviction of a man about to die. He saw the sword plunge toward his breast as . . .

. . . he gathered the light about him, sweeping his

hands through the dripping colors, making them shift and flow for him. He saw the figure of Krane, standing haughtily in the bank of yellow, and he gathered the blue to himself in a coruscating ball.

Fearsomely he bellowed his challenge, 'This is *my* illusion, Krane, and watch as I kill you!'

He balled the blue in his hand and sent it flying, dripping spark and color as it shot toward the black-bearded man.

They both stood tall and spraddle-legged in the immensity of they knew-not-where. The colors dripped from the air, making weird patterns as they mixed and ran.

The blue ball struck in front of Krane and exploded, cascading a rich flood of chromatic brilliance into the air. Krane laughed at the failure.

He gathered the black to him, wadding it in strong and supple fingers. He wound up, almost as though it was a sport, and flung the wadded black at Marmorth.

The older man knew he had not enough belief yet built to withstand this onslaught. Marmorth knew if the black enfolded him he would die in the never-ending limbo of nothingness.

He thrust hands up before his face to stop the onrush of the black, but it struck him and he fell, clutching feebly at a washy stringer of white.

He fell into the black as it surrounded him, and in a moment knew he was in the limbo.

This was not his illusion! It could not be, for he was vanquished! Yet he was not dead, as he had felt sure he would be. He lay there, thinking.

He remembered all the effort he had put in on the Political Theorem. The Theorem he had proposed in the Council. It had represented years of work—the culmination of all his adult thought and effort; and, he had to admit it, the Theorem was soundly based on his own view of the Universe.

Then the presumptuous Krane had offended him by restating the Theorem. Before the very faces of the Council!

Krane had, of course, twisted it to his own evil and malicious ends—basing it anew on *his* conception of the All.

Oh, there had been a verbal battle. There had been the accusations, the clanging of the electric gavel, the remonstrances of the Compjudge, the shocked expressions of the other Councilors! Till finally Marmorth had been goaded by the younger man into the Duel. Then into the Silver Corridor.

From which only one of them would emerge. The one who did would force his Theorem on the Council. To be accepted, of course. The Theorem was so basic, the view would be recognized and accepted.

It all revolved, then, around whose view of the Universe, whose Theorem, was the right one. It could be either Krane's or Marmorth's.

Marmorth struck out at the black! *Mine, mine, mine!* he shouted soundlessly. He lashed into the nothingness. *My Theorem is the proper one! I believe it! I do!*

Then he saw the stringer of white in his hand. So this was Krane in the ascendant, was it! Now came the moment of retaliation.

He whipped the stringer around his invisible head, swaying as he was, there in the depthless black. The stringer thickened. He cupped it to him, washing it with his hands, strengthening it, shaping and molding it.

In a moment, it had grown. In a moment more the white had burst forth like a ripe blossom and flooded all. Revealing Krane standing there, in his breechclout, massaging the pale pink between his fingers.

'Mine, Krane, *mine*!' he screamed, flinging the orange-green!

Krane blanched and tried to duck. The orange-green came on like a sliver of Forever, streaking and burning as it rode currents that did not exist. Then the light shattered, and fired, and spat. As Marmorth realized they had nullified each other again, that the illusion was dissolving around them, he heard Krane bellow, even as loud as *he* had, 'Mine, Marmorth, *mine*!'

Then the colors ran. They flowed, they merged, they sucked at his body, while he . . .

. . . shrank up against the glass wall next to Krane. They both stared in fascinated horror as the huge, ichor-dripping spider-thing advanced on them, mandibles clicking.

'My God in Heaven!' Marmorth heard Krane bellow. 'What is it?' Krane scrabbled at the glass wall behind them, trying to get out. They were trapped.

The glass walls circled them, wide; just the spider-thing and each other, trapped in the tiny tomb!

Marmorth was petrified. He could neither move nor speak—he could hardly sense anything but terror. Spiders were his personal fear. He found his legs were quivering at the knees, though he had not sensed it a moment before. The very sight of the hairy beasts had always sent shudders through him. Now he knew this was his illusion. *He* was in ascendant!

But how hideously in the ascendant.

The spider-thing advanced on them, the soft plush pads of its hundred feet leaving dampness where it stopped.

Krane fell to his knees, moaning and scratching at the glass floor. 'Out, out, out, out . . .' he mumbled, froth dripping from his lips.

Marmorth knew this was his chance. This fear was a product of his own mind; he had lived with it all his life. He knew it more familiarly than Krane—he could not cancel it, certainly, but he could utilize it more easily than the other.

Here was where he killed Krane. He pulled himself tightly to the wall, sweating palms flat to the glass, the valley of his backbone against the cool surface. 'I'm right! The Theorem as I stated it i-is c-correct!' He said it triumphantly, though the note of terror quavered undisguised in his voice.

The spider-thing paused in its march, swung its clicking, ghastly head about as though confused, and altered direction by an inch. Away from Marmorth. It descended on Krane.

The black-bearded man looked up, saw it coming toward him, heard Marmorth's words. Even on the floor, half-sunk in shock, he shouted, pounding his fists against the floor of glass, 'Wrong, wrong, wrong! You're wrong! I can prove *my* Theorem is correct! The basic formation of the Judiciary should be planned in an ever-decreasing system of——'

Marmorth didn't even listen. He knew it was drivel! He knew the man was wrong! But the spider-thing had stopped once more. Now it paused between the two of them, its bulk shivering as though caught in a draft.

Krane saw the hesitation on the monster's part, and rose, the old confidence and impudence regained. He wiped his balled fists across his eyes, clearing them of tears. He continued speaking, steadily, and to Marmorth's ears, in the voice of a fanatic. The man just could *not* recognize that he was wrong.

'You're insane, man!' Marmorth interjected, waving his hands with fervor. 'The setup must be balanced between a code of fair practices with a Guild system blocking efforts on the part of the Genres to rise into control of the gross planetary product!' He went on and on, outlining the Theorem.

Krane, too, shouted and gesticulated, both of them

suddenly oblivious to the monstrous, black spider-thing which had stopped completely between them, vacillating.

When Marmorth stopped for an instant to regain his breath, the beast twisted its neckless head toward him. Marmorth then speeded up his speech, spewing out detail upon detail, and the beast slowly sank back into uncertainty.

It was obviously a battle of belief. Whichever combatant had more conviction—that one would win.

They stood and shouted, screamed, outlined, explained and delineated for what seemed hours. Finally, as though in exasperation, the spider-thing began to turn. They both watched it, their mouths working, words pouring forth in twin streams of absolute sincere belief.

They watched even though . . .

. . . the starships fired at each other mercilessly. Blast after blast exploded soundlessly into the vault of space. Marmorth found his fingers twisted in the epaulet at his right shoulder.

As he watched Krane's *Magnificent-class* destroyer wheel in the control-room screens, a half-naked, blood-soaked and perspiring crewman burst into the cabin's entrance-well.

'Captain! Captain, sir!'

Marmorth looked over the plastic rail, down into the well.

'What?' His voice snapped with brittleness.

'Cap'n, the port side is riddled! We're losing pressure from thirteen compartments. The Reclamation Mile is completely lost! The engineers' group was in one of the compartments along that mile, Cap'n! They're all bloated and blue and dead in there! We can see them floating around without any . . .'

'*Get the Hell out of here!*' Marmorth turned, lifting a spacetant from his chart-board, and flinging it with all his strength at the crewman. The man ducked and the spacetant bounced off the bulkhead, snapping pieces from its intricate bulk.

'You maniac!' he yowled, leaping back out of the well, through the exit port, as Marmorth reached for another missile.

Marmorth shut his eyes tight, blanking out the shuddering ship, space, the screens, everything.

'Right, right, right, right, right! I'm right!' he shouted, lifting clenched fists.

The explosion came in two parts, as though two torpedoes had struck almost simultaneously. The ship rocked and heeled. Bits of metal sheared through the outer bulkheads, crashed against the opposite wall.

As the lights went dead, and the screams drove into his brain, Marmorth shouted his credo once more, with all the force of his conviction, with all the power of his lungs, with all the strength in his gasping body.

'I'm right! May God strike me dead if I'm not right! I know I'm right, I made an inexhaustible . . .'

. . . check!' he finished, opening his eyes and looking back down at the chessboard. The pieces, happily, had not moved. He still had Krane blocked off.

'I say check,' he repeated, smiling, steepling his fingers.

Krane's black-bearded face broke into a wry grimace.

'Most clever, my dear Marmorth,' he congratulated the other with sarcasm. 'You have forced me to touch a pawn.'

Marmorth watched as Krane, with trembling fingers, reached down to the jet pawn. It was carved from stone; carved with such care and intricacy that its edges were precisely as they had been desired by the master craftsman. They were razor sharp.

The pieces were all cut the same. Both the blanched

alabaster pieces before Marmorth, and the ebony-stone players under Krane's hand. The game had been constructed for men who played more than a 'gentleman's game.' There was death in each move.

Marmorth knew he was in the ascendant. Each of them had had two illusions—that remembrance was sharp—and this was Marmorth's. How did he know? The older man looked down at the intricately carved chess pieces. He was white, Krane was black. As clear as it could be.

'Uh, have you moved?' Marmorth inquired, his voice unctuous with casualness. He knew the other had not yet touched his players. 'I believe you still lie in check.' He was enjoying toying with his once-arrogant foe.

He thought he heard a muted, 'Damn you!' under Krane's breath, but could not be certain.

Slowly Krane touched the player, carefully sliding the fingers of his hand across the razor-thin, razor-sharp facets. The piece almost slid from his grasp, so loosely was he holding it, but the move was made in an instant.

Marmorth cursed mentally. Krane had calculated beautifully! Not only was his King blocked out from Marmorth's Rook—Marmorth's check-piece—but in another two moves (so clearly obvious as Krane had desired it) his own Queen would be in danger. In his mind he could hear Krane savoring the words: *'Gardé! I say gardé, my dear Marmorth!'*

He had to move the Queen out of position.

He had to touch the Queen!

The most deadly piece on the board!

'No!' he gasped.

'I beg your pardon?' said Krane, the slash-mouth opening in a violent grin.

'N-nothing, nothing!' snapped Marmorth. He concentrated. Deadly poison, instant-acting, lay filmed on those razor edges.

There was little chance he could maneuver that thousand-keen-edged Queen without poisoning himself for his trouble. Lord! It was an insoluble, a double-edged, dilemma. If he did not move, Krane would win. If he won, it was obvious Marmorth would die. He had seen the deadly dirk's hilt protruding slightly from Krane's cummerbund when the other had sat down. If he *did* move, he would convulse to death before Kane's taunting eyes.

You shall never have that pleasure! he thought, the bitter determination of a man who will not be defeated rising in him.

He approached the Queen, with hand, with eye.

The base was faceted, like a diamond. Each facet ended in a cutting edge so sensitive he knew it would sever the finger that touched it. The shape of the upper segments was involved, gorgeously-made. A woman, arms raised above her head, stretching in tension. Beautiful—and untouchable.

Then the thought struck him: *Is this the only move?*

Deep within his mind he calculated. He could not possibly recognize the levels on which his intellect was working. In with his chess theory, in with his mental agility, in with his desire to win, his Theorem rearranged itself, fitting its logic to this situation. How could the Theorem be applied to the game? What other paths, through the infallible truth of the Theorem—in which he believed, now, more strongly than ever before—what other paths could he take.

Then the alternative move became clear. He could escape a route, escape the *gardé*, escape the taunting smile of Krane by moving a relatively safe Bishop. It was not a completely foolproof action, since the Bishop, too, was a razored piece of death, but he had found a way around the certain success of Krane's maneuverings.

'Ha!' A terrible smile burst upon his face. His eyes

bored across to the other's. Krane turned white as Marmorth reached out, touched the one piece he had been desperately hoping the older man would not consider.

He felt the uncontrollable tightening in his throat as he realized the game would go on, and on, and on and...

...he unclenched his fist as the volcano leaped up around them.

It was more than the inside of a volcanic cone, however. The Corridor was there, too. The dung-brown walls of smooth rock shivered ever so slightly, and both men knew the Silver Corridor was just beyond their vision. They could see it glimmering with unreality.

It was almost as though they were looking at a double exposure; an extinct volcano superimposed over the shining tube of the Silver Corridor.

It isn't far away, thought Marmorth. *This must be the last illusion! Is there a certain pattern to these things?* Then he felt, with a blissed release of nervous tension, *Someone is going to win soon.*

He stared up at the faint patch of gray sky, visible through the roundly jagged opening at the cone's top. The walls sloped down in a fluid concavity. Here and there across the rough floor of the cavern, stalagmites rose up in sharp spikes.

And there—over and through the walls of the dead formations—the Corridor hung faintly. A ghostly, shivering, not-quite-real shadow, inside the substance of their illusion.

They stood and stared at each other. Each knowing he was not really in the heart of a volcano, but in a metal corridor. Each knowing he could die as easily by this illusion as he could at the other's hands.

Was this the end? Were there a limited number of illusions to each Affair? Who had won? Could there *be* a winner?

They stared at each other, across the dusky interior of the extinct volcano.

'I'm right,' said Krane, hesitantly.

'You're wrong,' answered Marmorth quickly. '*I'm* the one who's right!'

In a moment they were at it again, each screaming till his lungs were raw with the effort, and red patches had appeared in Marmorth's cheeks. They paused for an instant, gathering air for another tirade, Krane looking about for a weapon.

They were both as they had begun. Naked save the breechclouts which clung to their buttocks.

They resumed their shouting, the sound reverberating hollowly in the dim interior of the volcano. The sounds hit them, bounced across the stone walls, reverberated again. The fury had been built to a peak and pitch they both knew could not be exceeded. They had strained every last vestige of belief and conviction in their minds.

As Marmorth realized he was at the pinnacle of his belief, he saw the same conviction come over Krane's face. He knew that from here on in, it would be a physical thing, with both of them stalemated in illusory power.

Then the woman-thing appeared.

She grazed into being between them. She wasn't human. There was no question about that. Marmorth took a halting step backward. Krane remained rooted, though his pale face had blanched an even more deadly shade. A strangled, 'My God, what *is* it?' slipped past Marmorth's lips.

It was less than human, yet more than mortal; it was a travesty of a human being. A mad nightmare of a vision! Like some fearsome god of an ancient cult, it paused with long legs apart, hands on hips.

The woman's body was lush. Full, high breasts, trim stomach, exciting legs. Gorgeously proportioned and exciting, the torso and legs, the chest and arms, were normal—even exaggeratedly normal.

But there all resemblance to a woman ceased.

The head was a strangely lizardlike thing, with elongated snout, wattles, huge glowing eyes set atop the skull. Looking out through flesh-sockets thick and deep—little hummocks atop the face—the eyes were small, crimson and cruel.

The nose was almost nonexistent. Two breather-spaces pulsed, one on either side of a small rise in the yellowed, pocked flesh of the head.

The mouth was a wide, gaping, triangular orifice, with triple rows of shark teeth in the upper and lower jaws. The woman-thing looked like a gorgeous female—with the weirdly altered head of a crocodile.

The ebony, leathery, bat's wings rising from the shoulder blades—quivering—completed the frightening picture.

Wisps of smoky, filmy garments were draped over the woman-thing's shoulders, around her waist. She stood unmoving.

Then she spoke to them.

It was not mental. It actually sounded; but not from the body before them. They knew it was—her?—but it did not come from her at all. The fearful mouth remained almost shut, propped slightly open on the sharp tiers of teeth.

The voice issued from the walls, from the tips of the stalagmites, from the high, arching roof of the volcano; it boomed from the rocky floor—it even floated down the length of the infinitely-stretching Corridor.

The voice spoke in thunder, yet softly.

Well, Gentlemen?

Krane stared for a second at the woman-thing; then he looked about wildly, trying to find the source of the voice. His head swung back and forth as though it was manipulated by strings from above. 'Well, *what*?' he shouted to no one.

Have you realized the truth yet?

'What truth? What are you talking about? Who is that? Is it you?' chimed in Marmorth, bathed in sudden fear. He pointed an accusing finger at the woman-thing.

The Corridor shimmered oddly. It lived just behind the stone walls of the volcano.

I'm a voice, Gentlemen. A voice and an illusion. Just an illusion, that's all, Gentlemen. Just an illusion from both of your minds. Made of equal portions of your minds. For you are one as strong as the other.

There was a pause. Then:

But tell me, have you realized what you should have known before you were foolish enough to enter the Corridor?

Krane looked at Marmorth with suspicion. For the first time it occurred to him that perhaps this was a trick on the other's part. Marmorth, recognizing the glance, shrugged his shoulders eloquently. 'No! Tell us, then! *What* should we have known?'

The only real answer as to who is right; which Theorem is the correct one!

'Tell me, tell me!' they shouted, almost together.

There was silence for a moment. The woman-thing ran a scarlet-tipped hand across the hideous lizard snout, as though searching for a way to phrase what was coming. Then the single word sounded in the heart of the volcano.

Neither.

Krane and Marmorth stared past the woman-thing, stared at each other in confusion. 'N-neither?' shouted Marmorth incredulously. 'Are you mad! Of course one of us is right! Me!' He was shaking fists at the gruesome being before him. Illusion, perhaps; but an illusion that was goading him.

'Prove it! Prove it!' screamed Krane, stepping forward, flat-footedly, as though seeking to strike the woman-thing. Then the voice gave them the solution and the proof that neither could contest, for both knew it to be true on a level that defied mere conviction.

You are both egomaniacs. You could not possibly be convinced of the other's viewpoint. Not in a hundred million years. The message dies between you. You are both too tightly ensnared in yourselves!

The woman-thing suddenly began to shimmer. She became indistinct, and there were many shadow-forms of her, surrounding her body like halos. Abruptly, she disappeared from between them. Leaving them alone in the quickening darkness of the volcano's throat.

Alone. Staring at each other with dawning comprehension, dawning belief.

They both realized it at the same moment. They both had the conviction of their cause, yet they both knew the woman-thing had been right.

'Krane,' said Marmorth, starting toward the black-bearded man, 'she's right, you know. Perhaps we can get together and figure . . .'

The other had started toward the older man as he had spoken. 'Yes, perhaps there's something in what you say. Perhaps there's a . . .'

At the instant they both realized it—the instant they considered the other's viewpoint—the illusion barriers shattered, of course, and the red-hot lava poured in on them, engulfing both men in a blistering inferno.

'Repent, Harlequin!' Said the Ticktockman

There are always those who ask, what is it all about? For those who need to ask, for those who need points sharply made, who need to know 'where it's at,' this:

'The mass of men serve the state thus, not as men mainly, but as machines, with their bodies. They are the standing army, and the militia, jailors, constables, posse comitatus, etc. In most cases there is no free exercise whatever of the judgment or of the moral sense; but they put themselves on a level with wood and earth and stones; and wooden men can perhaps be manufactured that will serve the purpose as well. Such command no more respect than men of straw or a lump of dirt. They have the same sort of worth only as horses and dogs. Yet such as these even are commonly esteemed good citizens. Others—as most legislators, politicians, lawyers, ministers, and office-holders—serve the state chiefly with their heads; and, as they rarely make any moral distinctions, they are as likely to serve the Devil, without intending it, as God. A very few, as heroes, patriots, martyrs, reformers in the great sense, and *men*, serve the state with their consciences also, and so necessarily resist it for the most part; and they are commonly treated as enemies by it.

HENRY DAVID THOREAU
Civil Disobedience'

That is the heart of it. Now begin in the middle, and

later learn the beginning; the end will take care of itself.

But because it was the very world it was, the very world they had allowed it to *become*, for months his activities did not come to the alarmed attention of The Ones Who Kept The Machine Functioning Smoothly, the ones who poured the very best butter over the cams and mainsprings of the culture. Not until it had become obvious that somehow, someway, he had become a notoriety, a celebrity, perhaps even a hero for (what Officialdom inescapably tagged) 'an emotionally disturbed segment of the populace,' did they turn it over to the Ticktockman and his legal machinery. But by then, because it was the very world it was, and they had no way to predict he would happen—possibly a strain of disease long-defunct, now, suddenly, reborn in a system where immunity had been forgotten, had lapsed—he had been allowed to become too real. Now he had form and substance.

He had become a *personality*, something they had filtered out of the system many decades before. But there it was, and there *he* was, a very definitely imposing personality. In certain circles—middle-class circles—it was thought disgusting. Vulgar ostentation. Anarchistic. Shameful. In others, there was only snickering, those strata where thought is subjugated to form and ritual, niceties, proprieties. But down below, ah, down below, where the people always needed their saints and sinners, their bread and circuses, their heroes and villains, he was considered a Bolivar; a Napoleon; a Robin Hood; a Dick Bong (Ace of Aces); a Jesus; a Jomo Kenyatta.

And at the top—where, like socially attuned Shipwreck Kellys, every tremor and vibration threatening to dislodge the wealthy, powerful, and titled from their flagpoles—he was considered a menace; a heretic; a rebel; a disgrace; a peril. He was known down the line, to the very heartmeat core, but the important reactions were high above and far below. At the very top, at the very bottom.

So his file was turned over, along with his time card and his cardioplate, to the office of the Ticktockman.

The Ticktockman: very much over six feet tall, often silent, a soft purring man when things went timewise. The Ticktockman.

Even in the cubicles of hierarchy, where fear was generated, seldom suffered, he was called the Ticktockman. But no one called him that to his mask.

You don't call a man a hated name, not when that man, behind his mask, is capable of revoking the minutes, the hours, the days and nights, the years of your life. He was called the Master Timekeeper to his mask. It was safer that way.

'This is *what* he is,' said the Ticktockman with genuine softness, 'but not *who* he is. This time-card I'm holding in my left hand has a name on it, but it is the name of *what* he is, not *who* he is. The cardioplate here in my right hand is also named, but not whom named, merely what named. Before I can exercise proper revocation, I have to know who this what is.'

To his staff, all the ferrets, all the loggers, all the finks, all the commex, even the mineez, he said, 'Who is this Harlequin?'

He was not purring smoothly. Timewise, it was jangle.

However, it *was* the longest single speech they had ever heard him utter at one time, the staff, the ferrets, the loggers, the finks, the commex, but not the mineez, who usually weren't around to know, in any case. But even they scurried to find out.

Who is the Harlequin?

High above the third level of the city, he crouched on the humming aluminum-frame platform of the air-boat (foof! air-boat, indeed, swizzleskid is what it was, with a tow-rack jerry-rigged) and stared down at the neat Mondrian arrangement of the buildings.

Somewhere nearby, he could hear the metronomic left-right-left of the 2:47 P.M. shift, entering the Timkin roller-bearing plant, in their sneakers. A minute later, precisely, he heard the softer right-left-right of the 5:00 A.M. formation, going home.

An elfin grin spread across his tanned features, and his dimples appeared for a moment. Then, scratching at his thatch of auburn hair, he shrugged within his motley, as though girding himself for what came next, and threw the joystick forward, and bent into the wind as the air-boat dropped. He skimmed over a slidewalk, purposely dropping a few feet to crease the tassels of the ladies of fashion, and—inserting thumbs in large ears—he stuck out his tongue, rolled his eyes and went wugga-wugga-wugga. It was a minor diversion. One pedestrian skittered and tumbled, sending parcels everywhichway, another wet herself, a third keeled slantwise and the walk was stopped automatically by the servitors till she could be resuscitated. It was a minor diversion.

Then he swirled away on a vagrant breeze, and was gone. Hi-ho.

As he rounded the cornice of the Time-Motion Study Building, he saw the shift, just boarding the slidewalk. With practiced motion and an absolute conservation of movement, they sidestepped up onto the slowstrip and (in a chorus line reminiscent of a Busby Berkeley film of the antediluvian 1930's) advanced across the strips ostrich-walking till they were lined up on the expresstrip.

Once more, in anticipation, the elfin grin spread, and there was a tooth missing back there on the left side. He dipped, skimmed, and swooped over them; and then, scrunching about on the air-boat, he released the holding pins that fastened shut the ends of the homemade pouring troughs that kept his cargo from dumping prematurely. And as he pulled the trough-pins, the air-boat slid over the factory workers and one hundred and fifty thousand dollars' worth of jelly beans cascaded down on the expresstrip.

Jelly beans! Millions and billions of purples and yellows and greens and licorice and grape and raspberry and mint and round and smooth and crunchy outside and soft-mealy inside and sugary and bouncing jouncing tumbling clittering clattering skittering fell on the heads and shoulders and hardhats and carapaces of the Timkin workers, tinkling on the slidewalk and bouncing away and rolling about underfoot and filling the sky on their way down with all the colors of joy and childhood and holidays, coming down in a steady rain, a solid wash, a torrent of color and sweetness out of the sky from above, and entering a universe of sanity and metronomic order with quite-mad coocoo newness. Jelly beans!

The shift workers howled and laughed and were pelted, and broke ranks, and the yellow beans managed to work their way into the mechanism of the slidewalks after which there was a hideous scraping as the sound of a million fingernails rasped down a quarter of a million blackboards, followed by a coughing and a sputtering, and then the slidewalks all stopped and everyone was summarily dumped thisawayandthataway in a jackstraw tumble, still laughing and popping little jelly bean eggs of childish color into their mouths. It was a holiday, and a jollity, an absolute insanity, a giggle. But...

The shift was delayed seven minutes.

They did not get home for seven minutes.

The master schedule was thrown off by seven minutes.

Quotas were delayed by inoperative slidewalks for seven minutes.

He had tapped the first domino in the line, and one after another, like chik chik chik, the others had fallen.

The System had been seven minutes worth of disrupted. It was a tiny matter, one hardly worthy of note, but in a society where the single driving force was order and unity and promptness and clocklike precision and attention to the clock, reverence of the gods of the passage of time, it was a disaster of major importance.

So he was ordered to appear before the Ticktockman. It was broadcast across every channel of the communications web. He was ordered to be *there* at 7:00 dammit on time. And they waited, and they waited, but he didn't show up till almost ten-thirty, at which time he merely sang a little song about moonlight in a place no one had ever heard of, called Vermont, and vanished again. But they had all been waiting since seven, and it wrecked *hell* with their schedules. So the question remained: Who is the Harlequin?

But the *unasked* question (more important of the two) was: How did we get *in*to this position, where a laughing, irresponsible japer of jabberwocky and jive could disrupt our entire economic and cultural life with a hundred and fifty thousand dollars' worth of jelly beans...

Jelly for God's sake *beans!* This is madness! Where did he get the money to buy a hundred and fifty thousand dollars' worth of jelly beans? (They knew it would have cost that much, because they had a team of Situation Analysts pulled off another assignment, and rushed to the slidewalk scene to sweep up and count the candies, and produce findings, which disrupted *their* schedules and threw their entire branch at least a day behind.) Jelly beans! Jelly ... *beans*? Now wait a second—a second accounted for—no one has manufactured jelly beans for over a hundred years. Where did he get jelly beans?

That's another good question. More than likely it will never be answered to your complete satisfaction. But then, how many questions ever are?

The middle you know. Here is the beginning. How it

starts:

A desk pad. Day for day, and turn each day. 9:00—open the mail. 9:45—appointment with planning commision board. 10:30—discuss installation progress charts with J.L. 11:15—pray for rain. 12:00—lunch. *And so it goes.*

'I'm sorry, Miss Grant, but the time for interviews was set at 2:30, and it's almost five now. I'm sorry you're late, but those are the rules. You'll have to wait till next year to submit application for this college again.' *And so it goes.*

The 10:10 local stops at Cresthaven, Galesville, Tonawanda Junction, Selby and Farnhurst, but not at Indiana City, Lucasville and Colton, except on Sunday. The 10:35 express stops at Galesville, Selby and Indiana City, except on Sundays & Holidays, at which time it stops at ... *and so it goes.*

'I couldn't wait, Fred. I had to be at Pierre Cartain's by 3:00, and you said you'd meet me under the clock in the terminal at 2:45, and you weren't there, so I had to go on. You're always late, Fred. If you'd been there, we could have sewed it up together, but as it was, well, I took the order alone ...' *And so it goes.*

Dear Mr. and Mrs. Atterley: In reference to your son Gerald's constant tardiness, I am afraid we will have to suspend him from school unless some more reliable method can be instituted guaranteeing he will arrive at his classes on time. Granted he is an exemplary student, and his marks are high, his constant flouting of the schedules of this school make it impractical to maintain him in a system where the other children seem capable of getting where they are supposed to be on time *and so it goes.*

YOU CANNOT VOTE UNLESS YOU APPEAR AT 8:45 A.M.

'I don't care if the script is *good*. I need it Thursday!'

CHECK-OUT TIME IS 2:00 P.M.

'You got here late. The job's taken. Sorry.'

YOUR SALARY HAS BEEN DOCKED FOR TWENTY MINUTES TIME LOST.

'God, what time is it, I've gotta run!'

And so it goes. And so it goes. And so it goes. And so it goes goes goes goes goes tick tock tick tock tick tock and one day we no longer let time serve us, we serve time and we are slaves of the schedule, worshippers of the sun's passing, bound into a life predicated on restrictions because the system will not function if we don't keep the schedule tight.

Until it becomes more than a minor inconvenience to be late. It becomes a sin. Then a crime. Then a crime punishable by this:

EFFECTIVE 15 JULY 2389, 12:00 midnight, the office of the Master Timekeeper will require all citizens to submit their time-cards and cardioplates for processing. In accordance with Statute 555-7-SGH-999 governing the revocation of time per capita, all cardioplates will be keyed to the individual holder and——

What they had done was devise a method of curtailing the amount of life a person could have. If he was ten minutes late, he lost ten minutes of his life. An hour was proportionately worth more revocation. If someone was consistently tardy, he might find himself, on a Sunday night, receiving a communiqué from the Master Timekeeper that his time had run out, and he would be 'turned off' at high noon on Monday, please straighten your affairs, sir.

And so, by this simple scientific expedient (utilizing a scientific process held dearly secret by the Ticktockman's office) the System was maintained. It was the only expedient thing to do. It was, after all, patriotic. The schedules had to be met. After all, there *was* a war on!

But, wasn't there always?

'Now that is really disgusting,' the Harlqeuin said,

when pretty Alice showed him the wanted poster. 'Disgusting and *high*ly improbable. After all, this isn't the day of the desperado. A *wanted* poster!'

'You know,' Alice noted, 'you speak with a great deal of inflection.'

'I'm sorry,' said the Harlequin, humbly.

'No need to be sorry. You're always saying "I'm sorry." You have such massive guilt, Everett, it's really very sad.'

'I'm sorry,' he repeated, then pursed his lips so the dimples appeared momentarily. He hadn't wanted to say that at all. 'I have to go out again. I have to *do* something.'

Alice slammed her coffee-bulb down on the counter. 'Oh for God's *sake*, Everett, can't you stay home just *one* night! Must you always be out in that ghastly clown suit, running around an*noy*ing people?'

'I'm——' he stopped, and clapped the jester's hat onto his auburn thatch with a tiny tingling of bells. He rose, rinsed out his coffee-bulb at the tap, and put it into the drier for a moment. 'I have to go.'

She didn't answer. The faxbox was purring, and she pulled a sheet out, read it, threw it toward him on the counter. 'It's about you. Of course. You're ridiculous.'

He read it quickly. It said the Ticktockman was trying to locate him. He didn't care, he was going out to be late again. At the door, dredging for an exit line, he hurled back petulantly, 'Well, *you* speak with inflection, *too*!'

Alice rolled her pretty eyes heavenward. 'You're ridiculous.' The Harlequin stalked out, slamming the door, which sighed shut softly, and locked itself.

There was a gentle knock, and Alice got up with an exhalation of exasperated breath, and opened the door. He stood there. 'I'll be back about ten-thirty, okay?'

She pulled a rueful face. 'Why do you tell me that? Why? You *know* you'll be late! You *know* it! You're *always* late, so why do you tell me these dumb things? She closed the door.

On the other side, the Harlequin nodded to himself. *She's right. She's always right. I'll be late. I'm always late. Why do I tell her these dumb things?*

He shrugged again, and went off to be late once more.

He had fired off the firecracker rockets that said: I will attend the 115th annual International Medical Association Invocation at 6:00 P.M. precisely. I do hope you will all be able to join me.

The words had burned in the sky, and of course the authorities were there, lying in wait for him. They assumed, naturally, that he would be late. He arrived twenty minutes early, while they were setting up the spider-webs to trap and hold him, and blowing a large bullhorn, he frightened and unnerved them so, their own moisturized encirclement webs sucked closed, and they were hauled up, kicking and shrieking, high above the amphitheater's floor. The Harlequin laughed and laughed, and apologized profusely. The physicians, gathered in solemn conclave, roared with laughter, and accepted the Harlequin's apologies with exaggerated bowing and posturing, and a merry time was had by all, who thought the Harlequin was a regular foofaraw in fancy pants; all, that is, but the authorities, who had been sent out by the office of the Ticktockman, who hung there like so much dockside cargo, hauled up above the floor of the amphitheater in a most unseemly fashion.

(In another part of the same city where the Harlequin carried on his 'activities,' totally unrelated in every way to what concerns us here, save that it illustrates the Ticktockman's power and import, a man named Marshall Delahanty received his turn-off notice from the Ticktockman's office. His wife received the notification from the gray-suited mindee who delivered it, with the traditional 'look of sorrow' plastered hideously across his face. She knew what it was, even without unsealing it. It was a billet-doux of immediate recognition to everyone these days. She gasped, and held it as though it was a glass slide tinged with botulism, and prayed it was not for her. Let it be for Marsh, she thought, brutally, realistically, or one of the kids, but not for me, please dear God, not for me. And then she opened it, and it *was* for Marsh, and she was at one and the same time horrified and relieved. The next trooper in the line had caught the bullet. 'Marshall,' she screamed, 'Marshall! Termination, Marshall! OhmiGod, Marshall, whattl we do, whattl we do, Marshall, omigod-marshall...' and in their home that night was the sound of tearing paper and fear, and the stink of madness went up the flue and there was nothing, absolutely nothing they could do about it.

(But Marshall Delahanty tried to run. And early the next day, when turn-off time came, he was deep in the forest two hundred miles away, and the office of the Ticktockman blanked his cardioplate, and Marshall Delahanty keeled over, running, and his heart stopped, and the blood dried up on its way to his brain, and he was dead that's all. One light went out on his sector map in the office of the Master Timekeeper, while notification was entered for fax reproduction, and Georgette Delahanty's name was entered on the dole roles till she could remarry. Which is the end of the footnote, and all the point that need be made, except don't laugh, because that is what would happen to the Harlequin if ever the Ticktockman found out his real name. It isn't funny.)

The shopping level of the city was thronged with the Thursday-colors of the buyers. Women in canary yellow chitons and men in pseudo-Tyrolean outfits that were jade and leather and fit very tightly, save for the balloon pants.

When the Harlequin appeared on the still-being-constructed shell of the new Efficiency Shopping Center, his bullhorn to his elfishly-laughing lips, everyone pointed and stared, and he berated them:

'Why let them order you about? Why let them tell you to hurry and scurry like ants or maggots? Take your time! Saunter a while! Enjoy the sunshine, enjoy the breeze, let life carry you at your own pace! Don't be slaves of time, it's a helluva way to die, slowly, by degrees . . . down with the Ticktockman!'

Who's the nut? most of the shoppers wanted to know. Who's the nut oh wow I'm gonna be late I gotta run . . .

And the construction gang on the Shopping Center received an urgent order from the office of the Master Timekeeper that the dangerous criminal known as the Harlequin was atop their spire, and their aid was urgently needed in apprehending him. The work crew said no, they would lose time on their construction schedule, but the Ticktockman managed to pull the proper threads of governmental webbing, and they were told to cease work and catch that nitwit up there on the spire with the bullhorn. So a dozen and more burly workers began climbing into their construction platforms, releasing the a-grav plates, and rising toward the Harlequin.

After the debacle (in which, through the Harlequin's attention to personal safety, no one was seriously injured), the workers tried to reassemble and assault him again, but it was too late. He had vanished. It had attracted quite a crowd, however, and the shopping cycle was thrown off by hours, simply hours. The purchasing needs of the system were therefore falling behind, and so measures were taken to accelerate the cycle for the rest of the day, but it got bogged down and speeded up and they sold too many floatvalves and not nearly enough wagglers, which meant that the popli ratio was off, which made it necessary to rush cases and cases of spoiling Smash-O to stores that usually needed a case only every three or four hours. The shipments were bollixed, the trans-shipments were misrouted, and in the end, even the swizzleskid industries felt it.

'Don't come back till you have him!' the Ticktockman said, very quietly, very sincerely, extremely dangerously.

They used dogs. They used probes. They used cardioplate crossoffs. They used teepers. They used bribery. They used stiktytes. They used intimidation. They used torment. They used torture. They used finks. They used cops. They used search&seizure. They used fallaron. They used betterment incentive. They used fingerprints. They used Bertillon. They used cunning. They used guile. They used treachery. They used Raoul Mitgong, but he didn't help much. They used applied physics. They used techniques of criminology.

And what the hell: they caught him.

After all, his name was Everett C. Marm, and he wasn't much to begin with, except a man who had no sense of time.

'Repent, Harlequin!' said the Ticktockman.

'Get stuffed!' the Harlequin replied, sneering.

'You've been late a total of sixty-three years, five months, three weeks, two days, twelve hours, forty-one minutes, fifty-nine seconds, point oh three six one one one microseconds. You've used up everything you can, and more. I'm going to turn you off.'

'Scare someone else. I'd rather be dead than live in a dumb world with a bogey man like you.'

'It's my job.'

'You're full of it. You're a tyrant. You have no right to order people around and kill them if they show up late.'

'You can't adjust. You can't fit in.'

'Unstrap me, and I'll fit my fist into your mouth.'

'You're a nonconformist.'

'That didn't used to be a felony.'

'It is now. Live in the world around you.'

'I hate it. It's a terrible world.'

'Not everyone thinks so. Most people enjoy order.'

'I don't, and most of the people I know don't.'

'That's not true. How do you think we caught you?'

'I'm not interested.'

'A girl named pretty Alice told us who you were.'

'That's a lie.'

'It's true. You unnerve her. She wants to belong, she wants to conform, I'm going to turn you off.'

'Then do it already, and stop arguing with me.'

'I'm not going to turn you off.'

'You're an idiot!'

'Repent, Harlequin!' said the Ticktockman.

'Get stuffed.'

So they sent him to Coventry. And in Coventry they worked him over. It was just like what they did to Winston Smith in *1984*, which was a book none of them knew about, but the techniques are really quite ancient, and so they did it to Everett C. Marm, and one day quite a long time later, the Harlequin appeared on the communications web, appearing elfish and dimpled and bright-eyed, and not at all brainwashed, and he said he had been wrong, that it was a good, a very good thing indeed, to belong, and be right on time hip-ho and away we go, and everyone stared up at him on the public screens that covered an entire city block, and they said to themselves, well, you see, he was just a nut after all, and if that's the way the system is run, then let's do it that way, because it doesn't pay to fight city hall, or in this case, the Ticktockman. So Everett C. Marm was destroyed, which was a loss, because of what Thoreau said earlier, but you can't make an omelet without breaking a few eggs, and in every revolution, a few die who shouldn't, but they have to, because that's the way it happens, and if you make only a little change, then it seems to be worthwhile. Or, to make the point lucidly:

'Uh, excuse me, sir, I, uh, don't know how to uh, to uh, tell you this, but you were three minutes late. The schedule is a little, uh, bit off.'

He grinned sheepishly.

'That's ridiculous!' murmured the Ticktockman behind his mask: 'Check your watch.' And then he went into his office, going mrmee, mrmee, mrmee, mrmee.

Bright Eyes

Feet without toes. Softly padded feet, furred. Footsteps sounded gently, padding furry, down ink-chill corridors of the place. A place Bright Eyes had inhabited since before time had substance. Since before places had names. A dark place, a shadowed place, only a blot against the eternally nightened skies. No stars chip-ice twittered insanely against that night; for in truth the night was mad enough.

Night was a condition Bright Eyes understood. And he knew about day . . .

He knew about almost everything.

The worms. The moles. The trunks of dead trees. The whites of eggs. Music. And random sounds. The sound fish make in the deep. The flares of the sun. The scratch of unbleached cloth against flesh. The hounds that roamed the tundra. The way those who have hair see it go pale and stiff with age. Clocks and what they do. Ice cream. Wax seals on parchment dedications. Grass and leaves. Metal and wood. Up and down. Here and most of there. Bright Eyes knew it all.

And that was the reason his padding, acoustically-sussurating footsteps hissed high in the dark, beamed, silent corridors of the place. And why he would now, forever at last, make that long journey.

The giant rat, whose name was Thomas, lay curled, fetid, sleeping, near the great wooden gate; and as Bright

Eyes approached, it stirred. Then, like a mastiff, it lifted its bullet-shaped head, and the bright crimson eyes flickered artful awareness. The massive head stiffened on the neckless neck, and it shambled to its feet. The wire tail swished across hand-inset cobblestones, making scratching sounds in the silent night.

'It's time,' Bright Eyes murmured. 'Here, Thomas.' The great gray creature jogged to him, nuzzling Bright Eyes' leg. It sniffed at the net filled with old skulls, and its whiskers twitched like cilia for a moment.

Bright Eyes swung the great wooden gate open with difficulty, dislodging caked dirt and cold-hardened clots of stray matter. The heavy metal ring clanged as he dropped it against the portal. Then Bright Eyes swung to the back of the rat, and without reins or prompting, the rat whose name was Thomas, paced steadily through the opening, leaving behind the only home Bright Eyes had ever known, which he would never see again. There was mist on the land.

Strange and terrible portents had caused Bright Eyes to leave the place. Unwilling to believe what they implied, at first, Bright Eyes pursued the gentle patterns of his days—like all the other days he had ever known, alone. But finally, when the blood-red and gray colors washed in unholy mixture down the skies, he knew what had happened, and that it was his obligation to return to a place he had never seen, had only heard about from others, centuries before, and do what had to be done. The others were long-since dead: had been dead since before Christ took Barabbas' place on the cross. The place to which Bright Eyes must return had not even been known, had not even existed, when the others left the world. Yet it was Bright Eyes' place, by default, and his obligation to all the others who had passed before. Since he was the last of his kind, a race that had no name, and had dwelled in the castle-place for millennia, he only dimly understood what was demanded of him. Yet this he knew: the call had been made, the portents cast into the night to be seen by him; and he must go.

It was a journey whose length even Bright Eyes could not surmise. The mist seemed to cover the world in a soft shroud that promised little good luck on this mission.

And, inexplicably, to Bright Eyes, there was a crushing sadness in him. A sadness he did not fathom, could not plumb, dared not examine. His glowing sight pierced through the mist, as steadily and stately, Thomas moved toward Bright Eyes' final destination. And it would remain unknown, till he reached it.

Out of the mist the giant rat swung jauntily. They had passed among softly-rounded hills with water that dripped from above. Then the shoulders had become black rock, and gleaming pinpoints of diamond brilliance had shone in the rock, and Bright Eyes had realized they were in caves. But had they come from the land, inside . . . or had they come from some resting-land deep in the bowels of the Earth, into these less hidden caverns; and would they continue to another outside?

Far ahead, a dim light pulsed and glowed, and Bright Eyes spurred Thomas forward. The dim light grew more bold, more orange and yellow and menacing with sudden soft roars of bubbling thunder. And as they rounded the passage, the floor of the cave was gone, and in their path lay a boiling scar in the stone. A lava pit torn up out of the solid stone, hissing and bubbling fiercely with demonic abandon. The light burned at Bright Eyes, and the heat was gagging. The sour stench of sulphur bit at his senses, and he made to turn aside.

The giant rat suddenly bolted in panic, arching back, more like caterpillar than rodent, and Bright Eyes was tossed to the floor of the cave, his net of skulls rolling away from him. Thomas chittered in fear, and took steps away, then paused and returned to his master. Bright Eyes rose and patted the terrified beast several times. Thomas fell into quivering silence.

Bright Eyes retrieved the skulls. All but one, that had rolled across the stone floor and disappeared with a vagrant hiss into the flame-pit. The giant rat sniffed at the walls, first one, then the other, and settled against the far one. Bright Eyes contemplated the gash in the stone floor. It stretched completely across, and as far as he could tell, forward. Thomas chittered.

Bright Eyes looked away from the flames, into the fear-streaked eyes of the beast. 'Well, Thomas?' he asked. The rat's snout twitched, and it hunkered closer to the wall. It looked up at Bright Eyes imploringly. Bright Eyes came to the rat, crouched down, stroked its neat, tight fur. Bright Eyes brushed the wall. It was not hot. It was cool.

The rat knew.

Bright Eyes rose, walked back along the passage. He found the parallel corridor half a mile back in the direction they had come. Without turning, he knew Thomas had silently followed, and leading the way, he moved down the parallel corridor, in coolness. Even the Earth could not keep Bright Eyes from what had to be done.

They followed the corridor for a very long time, till the rock walls leaned inward, and the littered floor tilted toward the stalactite-spiked ceiling. Bright Eyes dismounted, and walked beside the giant rat. There were strange, soft murmurings beneath them. Thomas chittered every time the Earth rattled. Further on, the passage puckered narrower and narrower ... and Bright Eyes was forced to bend, then stoop, then crawl. Thomas slithered belly-tight behind him, more frightened to be left behind than to struggle forward.

A whisper of chill, clean air passed them.

They moved ahead, only the glow of Bright Eyes marking a passage.

Abruptly, the cave mouth opened onto darkness, and cold, and the world Bright Eyes had never seen, the world his dim ancestors had left, millenia before.

No one could ever set down what that first sight meant to Bright Eyes. But...

...the chill he felt, was not child of the night wind.

The countryside was a murmuring silence. The sky was so black, not even the stars seemed at home. Frightened, lonely and alienated from the universe they populated, the silver specks drifted down the night like chalk dust. And through the strangeness, Bright Eyes rode Thomas, neither seeing nor caring. Behind him a village passed over the horizon line, and he never knew he had been through it.

No shouts of halt were hurled on the wind. No one came to darkened windows to see Bright Eyes pass through. He was approaching there and gone, all in an instant of time that may have been forever and may have been never. He was a wraith on the mist-bottomed silence. And Thomas, moved stately through valley and village, only paced, nothing more. From now on, it was Bright Eyes' problem.

Far out on the plains, the wind opened up suddenly. It spun down out of the northwest and drove at Bright Eyes' back. And on the trembling coolness, the alien sounds of wild dogs came snapping across the emptiness. Bright Eyes looked up, and Thomas' neck hair bristled with fear. Bright Eyes stroked a round, palpitating ear and the great rat came under control.

Then, almost without sound that was tied to them—for the sound of dogs came from a distance, from far away—the insane beasts were upon them. A slavering band of crimson-eyed mongrels, some still wearing dog collars and clinking tags, hair grown shaggy and matted with filth. Noses with large nostrils, as though they had had to learn to forage the land all at once, rather than from birth. These were the dogs of the people, driven out onto the wind, to live or die or eat each other as best they could.

The first few leaped from ten feet away, high and flat in trajectories that brought them down on Thomas' back, almost into Bright Eyes' lap, their yellow teeth scraping and clattering like dice on cement, lunacy bubbling out of them as froth and stench and spastic claw-scrabblings. Thomas reared and Bright Eyes slid off without losing balance, using the bag of skulls as a mace to ward off the first of the vicious assaults. One great Doberman had its teeth set for a strike into Thomas' belly, but the great rat—with incredible ferocity and skill—snapped its head down in a scythelike movement, and rent the gray-brown beast from jowl to chest, and it fell away, bleeding, moaning piteously.

And the rest of the pack materialized from the darkness. Dozens of them, circling warily now that one of their number lay in a trembling-wet garbage heap of its own innards.

Bright Eyes whistled Thomas to him with a soft sound. They stood together, facing the horde, and Bright Eyes called up a talent his race had not been forced to use in uncounted centuries.

The great white eyes glowed, deep and bubbling as cauldrons of lava, and a hollow moaning came from a place deep in Bright Eyes' throat. A sound of torment, a sound of fear, an evocation of gods that were dust before the Earth began to gather moisture to itself in the senseless cosmos, before the Moon had cooled, before the patterns of magnetism had settled the planets of the Solar System in their sockets.

Out of that sound, the basic fiber of emotion, like some great machine phasing toward top-point efficiency, Bright Eyes drew himself tight and unleashed the blast of pure power at the dogs.

Buried deep in his mind, the key to pure fear as a weapon was depressed, and in a blinding fan of sweeping brilliance, the emotion washed out toward the horde, a comber of undiluted, unbuffered terror. For the first time in centuries, that immense power was unleashed. Bright Eyes *thought* them terrified, and the air stank with fear.

The dogs, bulge-eyed and hysterical, fled in a wave of yipping, trembling, tuck-tailed quivering.

As if the night could no longer contain the immensity of it, the shimmering sound of terror bulged and grew, seeking release in perhaps another dimension, some higher threshold of audibility, and finding none—it wisped away in darkness and was gone.

Bright Eyes stood trembling uncontrollably, every fiber of his body spasming. His pineal gland throbbed. An intracranial tumor—whose presence in a human brain would have meant death—absolutely imperative for Bright Eyes' coordinated thought processes, which had swollen to five times its size as he concentrated, till his left temple had bulged with the pressing growth of it—now shrank, subsided, sucked itself back down into the gray brain matter, the gliomas itself. And slowly, as the banked fires of his eyes softened once more, Bright Eyes came back to full possession of himself.

'It has been a very long time since that was needed,' he said gently, and dwelt for a moment on the powers his race had possessed, powers long-since gone to forgetfulness.

Now that it was over, the giant rat settled to the ground, licking at its fur, at a slash in the flesh where one of the mad things had ripped and found meat.

Bright Eyes went to him. 'They are the saddest creatures of all. They are alone.' Thomas continued licking at his wounds.

Days later, but closer to their final destination, they came to the edge of a great river. At one time it had been a swiftly-moving stream, whipping itself high in a pounding torrent filled with colors and sounds; but now it flushed itself to the sea wearily, riding low in its own tide-trough, and hampered by the log-jam. The log-jam was made of corpses.

Bodies, hideously bloated and maggot-white puffed out of human shapes, lay across one another, from the near shore to the opposite bank. Thousands of bodies, uncountable thousands, twisted and piled and washed together till it would have been possible to cross the river on the top layer of naked men's faces, bleached women's backs, twisted children's hands crinkled as if left too long in water. For they had been.

As far upstream as Bright Eyes could see, and as far downstream as the bend of the banks permitted, it was the same. No movement, save the very seldom jiggle of a corpse as the water passed through. For they were packed so deeply and so tightly that in truth only water at its most sluggish could wanly press through. Yet the water gurgled and twittered among them, stealing slowly downstream—caressing rotting flesh in obscene parody: water, cleansing steppingstones; polishing and smoothing and drenching them senselessly as it marks its passage only by what is left behind.

That was the ultimate horror of this river of dead: that the tide—no matter how held-back now—continued unheeding as it had since the world was born. For the world went on. And did not care.

Bright Eyes stood silently. At the bottom of the short slope that ended with shoreline, bodies were strewn in a careless tumble. He breathed very deeply, fighting for air and the shivering started again. As it grew more pronounced, there was movement in the dry-moist river bed. Bodies abruptly began to move. They trembled as though roiling in a stream growing turbulent. Then, one by one, they rearranged themselves. All up and down the length of the river, the bodies shifted and moved and lifted without aid from their original positions, and far off, where their movement to neatness could not be seen, there came the roar of dammed-up water breaking free, surging forward, freed from its restraining walls of once-human flesh.

As Bright Eyes trembled, power surging through his slight frame, his eyes seeming to wax and wane with currents of electricity, the river of corpses freed itself from its log-jam, and was open once more.

The water poured in a great frothing wave down and down the corpse-bordered trough of the river. It broke out of a box-canyon to Bright Eyes' left, like a wild creature penned too long and at last set free on the wind. It came bubbling, boiling, thrashing forward, passed the spot where he stood, and hurled itself away around the bend in the shoreline.

As Bright Eyes felt the trembling pass, the river rose, and rose, and gently now, rose. Covering the ghastly residue of humanity that now lay submerged beneath the mud-blackened waters.

The eyes of the trembling creature, the eyes of the giant rat, the eyes of the uncaring day were blessedly relieved of the sight of decay and death.

Emotions washed quickly, one after another, down his features; washed as quickly as the river had concealed its sad wealth; colors of sadness, imprinted in a manner no human being could ever have conceived, for the face that supported these emotions was of a race that had vanished before man had walked the Earth.

Then Bright Eyes turned, and with the rat, walked upstream. Toward the morning.

When the bleeding birds went over, the sun darkened. Great irregular, hard-edged clouds of them, all species, all wingspreads—but silent. Passing across the broad, gray brow of the sky, heading absolutely nowhere, they turned off the sun. It was suddenly chill as a crypt. Heading east. Not toward warmth, or instinct, or destination ... just anywhere, nowhere. Until they wearied, expired, dropped. Not manna, garbage. Live garbage that fell in hundredclots from the beat-winged flights.

Many dropped, fluttering idly as if too weary to fight the air currents any longer. As though what tiny instinctual brain substance they had possessed, were now baked, turned to jelly, squashed by an unnameable force into an ichorous juice that ran out through their eyes. As though they no longer cared to live, much less to continue this senseless flight east to nowhere...

...and they bled.

A rain of bird's blood, sick and discolored. It misted down, beading Bright Eyes, and the stiff rat fur, and the trees, and the still, silent, dark land.

Only the dead, flat no-sound of millions of wings metronomically beating, beating, beating...

Bright Eyes shuddered, turned his face from the sight above, and finding himself unable to look, yet unable to end the horror as he had the mad dogs or the water of corpses, sought surcease in his own personal vision.

And this, which had driven him forth, was his vision.

Sleeping, deep in that place where he had lived so long, Bright Eyes had felt the subtle altering of tempo in the air around him. It was nothing as obvious as machinery beginning to whirr, trembling the walls around him; nor as complex as a shift in dimensional orientation. It was, rather, a soft sliding in the molecules of everything except Bright Eyes. For an instant everything went just slightly out of synch, a little fuzzy, and Bright Eyes came awake sharply. The *thing* that had occurred, was something his race had pre-set eons before. It was triggered to activate itself—whatever 'itself' was—after certain events had *possibly* happened.

The fact that this shifting had occurred, made Bright Eyes grow cold and wary. He had expected to die without its ever having come. But now, this was the time, and it *had* happened, and he waited for the next phase.

It came quickly. The vision.

The air before him grew even more indistinct, more roiled, like a pool of quicksilver smoke trumbling in and in on itself. And from that cloudiness the image of the last of the Castellans took shape. (Was it image, or reality, or thought within his head? He did not really know, for Bright Eyes was merely the last of his kind, no specially-trained adept, and much of what his race had been, and knew, was lost to him, beyond him.)

The Castellan was a fifth-degree adept, and surely the last remaining one of Bright Eyes' race to—go. He wore the purple and blue of royalty, from a House Bright Eyes did not recognize, but the cut of the robe was shorter than styles Bright Eyes recalled as having been current—then. And the Castellan's cowl was up, revealing a face that was bleak with sorrow and even a hint of cruelty. Such was not present, of course, for the Castellans merely performed their duties, but Bright Eyes was certain *this* adept had been against the decision to—go. Yet he had been chosen to bring the message to Bright Eyes.

He stood, booted and silent, in the soft-washed blue and white lightness of Bright Eyes' sleeping chamber. Bright Eyes was given time to come to full wakefulness, and then the Castellan spoke.

'What you see has been gone for ten centuries. I am

the last, save you. They have set me the task, and this twist of my being, of telling you what you must do. If the proper portents trigger my twist to appear before you—pray it never happens—then you must go to the city of the ones with hair, the ones who come after us, the ones who inherit the Earth, the men. Go to their city, with a bag of skulls of our race. You will know what to do with them.

'Know this, Bright Eyes: we go voluntarily. Some of us—and I am one of them—more reluctantly than most. It is a decision that seems only proper. Those who come after us, Men, will have their chance for the stars. This was the only gift of birth we could offer. No other gift can have meaning between us. They must have our chance, so we have gone to the place where you now lie. By the time I appear to you—if ever I do—we will be gone. This is the way of it, a sad and an inescapable way. You will be the last. And now I will show you a thing.'

The Castellan raised his hands before his face, and as though they were growing transparent, they glowed with an inner fire. The Visioning power. The Castellan's face suffused with flames as it conjured up the proper vision for Bright Eyes.

It appeared out of lines of blossoming crimson force, in the very air beside the Castellan. A vision of terror and destruction. Flames man-made and devastating, incredible in their hellfire. Like some great arachnid of pure force, the demon flames of the destruction swept and washed across the vision, and when it faded, Bright Eyes lay shaken by what he had seen.

'If this that I have showed you ever comes to pass, then my twist will appear to you. And if you ever hear me as you hear me now, then go, with the bag of skulls of our people. And do not doubt your feelings.

'For if I appear to you, it will all have been in vain,

and those of us who were less pure in our motivations, will have been proved right.'

Shimmering substance, coalescing nothingness, air that trembled and twittered in reforming, and the Castellan was gone. Bright Eyes rose, and gathered the skulls from the crypt. Then:

Feet without toes. Softly-padded feet, furred. Footsteps sounded gently, padding furry, down ink-chill corridors of the place. A place Bright Eyes had inhabited since before time had substance. He walked through night, out of the place.

Night was a condition Bright Eyes understood. And he knew about day...

The bleeding birds were long since gone. Bright Eyes moved through the days, and onward. At one point he passed through a sector of trembling mountains that heaved up great slabs of rock and hurled them away like epileptics ridding themselves of clothes. The ground trembled and burst and screamed and the very earth went insane to tunes of destruction it had never written.

There was a plain of dead grass, sere and wasted with great heaps of desiccated insects heaped here, there. They had flocked together to the last resting-place, and the plain of dead grass was poor tapestry indeed to hold the imprisoned pigments of their dead flesh, the acrid and bittersweet pervasive odor of formic acid that lingered like hot breath of a mad giant across the silent windless emptiness. Yet, how faint, a sound of weeping...?

Finally, Bright Eyes came to the city.

Thomas would not enter. The twisted rope-pillars of smoke that still climbed relentlessly to the dark sky; the terrible sounds of steel cracking and masonry falling into empty streets; the charnel house odor. Thomas would not go in.

But Bright Eyes was compelled to enter. Into that last debacle of all. From where it had begun.

The dead were everywhere, sighing soundlessly with milk-white eyes at a tomorrow that had never come. And each fallen one soundlessly spoke the question of why. Bright Eyes walked with the burden of chaos pulsing in him. This. This is what it had come to.

For this, his race had gone away. That the ones with hair, the Men they had been called, they had called themselves, could stride the Earth. How cheap they had left it all. How cheap, how thin, how sordid. This was the last of it, the last of the race of men. Dust and dead.

Down a street, woman pleading out of death for mercy.

Through what had been a park, old men humped crazily in rigorous failure to escape.

Past a structure, building front ripped away as if fingernails had shorn it clean. Children's arms, pocked and burned, dangling. Tiny hands.

To another place. Not like the place from which Bright Eyes had come, but the place to which he had journeyed. No special marker, just . . . a place. Sufficient.

And then it was, that Bright Eyes sank to his knees, crying. Tears that had not been seen since before Man had come from caves, tears that Bright Eyes had never known. Infinite sadness. Cried. Cried for the ghosts of the creatures with hair, cried for Men. For Man. Each Man. The Man who had done away with himself so absurdly, so completely. Bright Eyes, on his knees, sorrowing for the ones who had lived here, and were gone, leaving him to the night, and the silence, and eternity. A melody never to be heard again.

He placed the skulls. Down in the soft white ash. Unresponsive, dying Earth, receiving its burden testament.

Bright Eyes, last of a race that had condemned itself to extinction, had condemned *him* to living in darkness forever, and had had only the saving wistful knowledge that the race coming after would live in the world. But now, gone, all of them, taking the world with them, leaving instead—no fair exchange—charnel house.

And Bright Eyes; alone.

Not only *their* race had been destroyed, in vain, but *his*, centuries turned to mud and diamonds in their markerless graves, had passed in futility. It had all, all of it, been for nothing.

So Bright Eyes—never Man—was the last man on Earth. Keeper of a silent graveyard; echoless tomb monument to the foolishness, the absurdity, of nobility.